AVARICE

CHARITY DEACON INVESTIGATIONS BOOK 4

P. A. WILSON

FREE EBOOK

Claim your copy of Buying Into Death when you use the QR code to sign up for my newsletter and follow Charity as she solves her fastest case yet!

ONE

My name is Charity Deacon and I'm a PI at my own agency — or half agency since I'd made Matthieu my partner. These days, my life flowed from boring to dangerous. It was better than before, when it just flowed from day-to-day. I became a private investigator when I got caught up in a case a few years ago. I'd seen something at an accident that the cops hadn't. Then, somehow Val Wei had come knocking at my door the same day begging me to help find her missing sister. One minute I didn't know any teenage prostitutes the next, I had one following me around to make sure I paid attention to her case.

Before I knew it, I was deep in the world of gangs and people traffickers. I guess I'm lucky that my... boyfriend, I hate that word, doesn't try to stop me from getting in too deep.

Now, here I was sitting at my kitchen table looking at a case-load of files and feeling pretty professional.

Business was slow. It was a perfect time for Matthieu and Lu to plan their wedding. So, he'd taken a few days off. I wasn't worried; I could manage the outstanding cases. I loved calling it that. PI's took cases, not just jobs. And I had a bit of capacity to take on another small one if I wanted to.

Or, I could just enjoy the break. It's not like I hate the private investigation business; it's a great gig for a woman with a pushy personality. I just like taking breaks as much as making money. The problem right now was Jake, that boyfriend I mentioned. His acting career was taking off, but it always took him away, and because of the current cases, I couldn't hop a plane to Australia and join him.

I stacked the six current files on the dining table and decided to get productive; sitting around was just making me antsy. The first file was an embezzlement case. If I'm going to be professional, I guess it's an alleged embezzlement. A page into the file and Matthieu's notes changed my mind; hidden assets, and an expensive girlfriend — the target was guilty. All that I had to do was write up the report and send it with the final invoice.

The next two files, both Matthieu's, were on hold until the clients contacted us to do the background checks. We did a fair amount of those for private colleges and hospitals. That left three of my own files. None of them were as organized as Matthieu's, but I knew exactly what was going on.

The warehouse: a few too many items falling off the back of a truck. I'd take pictures tonight, like I had three nights in a row. Eventually either I'd find evidence, or the client would close the case because I couldn't find any. The estate file: I had to track down a missing heir. Something I could do online and in my Pjs.

The final one was the most interesting. Sara Lyman, missing wife. The cops had written her off as a runaway. She wasn't a kid and wasn't in a high-risk position to be murdered. People ran away all the time. I'd followed a money trail for a couple of days, and then the clues stopped. I needed to find another track. I was pretty sure there was more to it than a bad marriage. Maybe I could talk to her coworkers. I had that information scribbled on a scrap of notepaper.

So, far from having a heavy case load, I had a few hour's effort to close the cases. If I worked at it, I might be able to take a couple of days off.

I signed on to a few databases to put in some queries on the wife and the heir, turned on the coffee maker, and settled in for the afternoon.

Then someone knocked on my door.

It's not that easy to get to my door. I live in a floating home in Vancouver's Coal Harbour. Our little community of five floating homes was kept behind a security gate. Since I hadn't let anyone in through the gate, it could only be one of my neighbors, or Val, who never seemed to need a key or to be buzzed in.

I opened the door, hoping it wasn't Delores, the self-appointed neighborhood watch.

It was Iain. He lived in the last house on the finger dock, next to Jake's. He'd been there about six months. All I knew about him was that he had a friendly chocolate lab named Mickey and worked in some high-tech conglomerate. He looked the part. A little bit taller than me, and I'm tall for a woman at 5 feet 8 inches. A runner's body, but I've never seen him head off or return from a run. He'd be hard to pick out in a crowd because he's average. Brown hair, brown eyes, wears the not-quite-executive look; dark gray slacks white shirt and a dark blue tie. I guessed that he must be on a coffee break, or he goes in late to work.

"Hey, Charity," he said. Then nothing.

He'd obviously knocked for a reason, and now I was going to have to get it out of him. "Iain, is there something I can help you with?" Not original, but a gal has to keep things moving.

"Delores said you might help me."

He looked over my shoulder into my house, and I knew it would be faster if I invited him in so he could feel comfortable.

Thankful that I hadn't changed into my PJs yet, I opened

the door wider. "I have a few minutes, why don't you come inside."

He took one of the armchairs in my living room. Okay, I call it the living room, but it's more like a living area. Two chairs and a small couch sat around a coffee table, no room for anything else.

I waited a few minutes while Iain looked around him. I'd been in his house. It was smaller than mine, so he couldn't be feeling cramped.

He was going to be one of those clients. Some people know they need your help, but they are embarrassed, or feeling guilty, so they don't like to come out and state the facts.

"Delores thinks you need my help?" I prompted, but he just nodded. "I'm a private investigator, so you must need something investigated?"

He sighed, then straightened from his slouch and started to talk. "Mickey has been kidnapped. I guess I mean dognapped." He shook his head when I started to say I wasn't that kind of PI. "I know it's not a big case, but he's important to me. I need him back and I don't know what to do."

TWO

He was almost in tears. I'm a sucker for a sad tale. I did not want to run around town looking for a lost dog, but maybe this dognapping would be more interesting than what I had on my plate. And how long could it take? "How do you know he's been taken? Maybe he just ran off and when he's bored, he'll come back."

Iain dug into his pocket and pulled out a wrinkled sheet of paper. "I got this stuffed into my mailbox."

It was a printout of a ransom note. Whoever had taken Mickey made it look like the letters came from newspaper clippings. Did they have a sense of humor? Or, didn't they know how to use a computer?

You want your dog back; we want five hundred bucks. If you don't pay the dog is never coming home.

Nothing else.

"Are you going to pay?"

He wiped his eyes, catching tears before they ran. There's a line between wimp and caring and Iain was getting close to the wimpy side of it. "I will, but they haven't told me where to go," he said.

"When did you get this?" I asked holding the note out.

"It was in my mailbox when I came home for lunch. So, ten minutes ago. Delores was there when I got it. I came right here."

If the dognappers were smart they would drop off another note or reach out some other way soon. They were asking a decent amount, something most people could afford if they had a dog. I had a feeling that Mickey wasn't their first victim.

"If you plan to pay, what do you want me to do?"

"I want you to find out who they are. I need Mickey back, and I don't want to wait. I can't take the risk that they'll take my money and keep him."

He'd lost his wimpy attitude. I got the feeling Mickey was more than just a pet.

I did not want to do this. It's not like I hate dogs, I just like humans better. Two missing people were waiting for my attention. If things went as I expected, Iain would get another note before the end of the day, and then he could pay the ransom. The problem is Iain's my neighbor, and if anything happened to his dog because I wouldn't help, I'd have to face that guilt every time I saw him.

Time for a compromise. "Do you have anything I can use as a clue? Like how they got Mickey in the first place?"

"He was in Dog Heaven. You know that spa on Georgia Street? When I got the note, I called. They said he'd been picked up by my brother. I don't have a brother. And I gave them an earful about their lack of security. Maybe they are in on it? You could start there."

Barging into a dog daycare and accusing the owners of a crime wasn't the best way to get information; especially if they called it a spa. But if I took the case, at least I had a lead. That was if I took the case. "Okay, Iain, here's the deal. I'm sure you'll get the instructions by the end of the day. Go get the cash.

When they call, come see me again. We'll figure out what to do."

He pushed himself up from the chair and reached out to shake my hand. "I feel better now with you on it. What's the fee?"

I hadn't taken the case, but I didn't want to argue it with him because I hadn't refused it either. "We'll talk fees when you hear from the dognappers. Maybe you won't need me."

I walked him the four steps to my door and watched him return to his house. I wasn't going to take on this case. I'd help him with paying the ransom and even with reporting the crime, but I had no time to track down anyone who kidnapped dogs for a living.

I WAS STILL FEELING KIND OF ANNOYED at Iain's request a couple of hours later. It was that kind of irritation that comes when someone asks you to do a favor, and says you can say no, but really the guilt at denying them is far more than the inconvenience of actually doing the favor. Then you get all mad that you feel guilty, and that they asked, and eventually you know you'll probably do it, but you have to stew for a while.

I'd set some searches going on the missing spouse and the lost heir. Most people who tried to disappear made some kind of mistake. I'd find a visa charge, or something that put me on the path. So, for the wife, I'd used both her married and maiden names. For the heir, I was pretty sure he wasn't trying to be lost. That one would be a matter of finding the one link that led to his door. When people disappeared and didn't get found... well it was more likely that they were dead than really good at hiding their tracks.

My phone buzzed as I got up to make a pot of coffee.

"Deacon Investigations." Maybe I'd change the name to

Deacon and Durand Investigations as a wedding present to Lu and Matthieu.

"I need someone who has experience with data loss." The voice was male, well spoken, no accent.

"That covers a lot. Can you give me more details?" Like a name? I usually didn't get the kind of client who kept things like that secret.

"Data security. That's all I can tell you right now."

Was this CISIS? CIA? NSA? Some other top secret, black ops organization? Probably just some small-time guy who lost a USB.

"Let's start with your name, then."

He sighed. "I said I can't tell you any details. Do you have experience with data loss?" Now he was pissed, and that seemed unwarranted.

"I don't work with anyone who doesn't trust me with his name."

"It's better that you don't know," he said. "Are you able to manage a case like this?"

Like what, asshole?

"Without details, I can't answer that question. If you have had a security breach, you need to contact someone with that expertise. I can give you some names."

"I don't want names. You come recommended."

"By who?" I really doubted that anyone I knew would recommend me for a data security job. I could set up some basic searches, and maybe hack through some simple features, but I wasn't a tech wiz.

"Can you help me?" He sounded desperate. Well, mad and desperate. That kind of client was more trouble than profit.

"No. Without details, I can't tell if we have the right skills. Would you like me to give you a few names that might be better suited?"

"So, you know enough to refer me, but you don't know enough to help me." He sneered the words.

Nasty.

"That's right. I'm sure you have more important things to do than argue with me." I wasn't going to waste any more of my time either. After all, I could be out dealing with dognappers.

He disconnected.

My irritation at Iain was gone. In its place was a gut twisting feeling that I should be afraid. Nothing the caller said was clearly menacing, but the whole call was off. I'd been threatened before, but never so oddly.

THREE

I checked my phone log, not expecting anything, the caller ID showed 'unknown'. My skills did extend to digging into phone records thanks to a friend who'd spent time training me.

I ran the program and found the cell towers involved. He was either in downtown Vancouver, Milwaukee, or Copenhagen. He knew how to bounce his signals, why did he need help with his data?

Ever since the time Peter Wong broke in and promised to finish the job he'd started by beating me up, I had high security on my home. Of course, a floating home could only be made so secure. And this guy seemed paranoid enough that he'd come after me if anything went wrong. I was smart to brush him off. I hoped.

My laptop pinged.

There was a result on the missing heir, maybe I'd get a payday and a closed case. Nice.

The target of my search was Tony Waterston. He was in line to inherit about a million dollars. Until I found him, the other two heirs got nothing. Mr. Waterston had broken with his family twenty years ago, after a nasty argument with his father, now deceased. His father had apparently forgiven Tony, but possibly Tony hadn't reciprocated. Anyway, there was a marriage license in Kentucky for Tony Waterston and Melissa Branch. I emailed the contact information to the estate lawyer. I'd been expressly forbidden to make contact with any of the potential Tony Waterstons. Part of me wondered what the family argument had been about, and another part didn't care.

Nothing on the Sara Lyman case yet.

I was getting bored. It was too early to go take pictures at the warehouse. It was just after 5 a.m. in Jake's time zone; either too late or too early for me to call him. I shouldn't call Lu. She was in full bride mode and anything not related to invitations, menus, or dresses made her more crazy. Maybe Val would be free for a coffee. Her organizing business was doing great, and the best part was that she managed her time like I did — taking time for fun too.

Before I could make the call, my phone rang and in one of those coincidences that people think are psychic powers, it was Val.

"Hey."

"How's it going?" She wanted something. This opening always ended in me doing her a favor. Before she became a businesswoman, Val was more direct. I guess she learned the same thing we all do; you can't just jump in to the topic when you are in business. People want the small talk.

"Busy, I'm hoping you can come with me tonight on a case." Maybe if I got my favor in first, I'd get it.

"Um."

No luck. She wasn't going to hear anything about my problems until I heard her out. Maybe it's a teenage thing. Or, maybe it was just a Val thing.

"What do you need, Val?"

"Okay. So, Rory and I are thinking about moving in together

and I don't know if it's a good idea, and I thought you could help me decide." She ended the rattling speech with a deep breath.

I don't like to get involved in big romantic decisions for my friends. Mainly because I didn't have my own act together. Jake and I spent so much time apart that we didn't have much in the way of conversations about a future. When Matthieu and Lu got together we were on a case in France. I just gave her a little push in his direction, but no advice. They'd worked it out all by themselves. Now, Matthieu was here and would soon be a married man. But they were both adults. Val didn't have any friends her age, and her sister wasn't around, maybe I should be helping her to make friends rather than just relying on me.

"I don't know, Val. I'm kind of busy here. Remember I was going to ask you for help?"

"Fine, what?"

Now she was getting pissy. It wouldn't make me give her advice and she knew that.

I told her about the case at the warehouse.

"So, you know how to skulk and take pictures. Why do you need me?"

I heard the front door open and looked up to see Val standing in my living room. The girl never had a problem getting past the security gate. She'd refused to take a key because she liked the challenge. And she said it would point out how people didn't follow the rules. Like she ever followed rules.

I disconnected and went to the kitchen. This was going to be harder face to face.

She walked over and started flipping through the files on my desk. "I thought you were busy? These are all on hold or waiting for a search response."

I handed her a diet soda and flipped the files closed. "If you aren't in the mood to help, you don't get to look at client information."

She laughed. "Fine. But I'm right, you weren't too busy. You have time to talk, right?"

I shook my head. "I got another case this morning." Maybe I hadn't said yes to Iain, but Val didn't know that.

She flopped onto the sofa. "Really? Something juicy? Like a murder? It's been a while."

I shouldn't have mentioned Iain's case. This was going to be embarrassing. "Yeah, and you remember how long it took for us to heal from the last murder. I don't want any more of those cases."

"So, what's it about? This case that means you don't have time to give me advice?" She pouted, but it didn't convince me. Val wasn't that kind of moody.

"If you don't have time to help me, why do you want to know?" If I could distract her from the question, maybe I wouldn't have to mention the dognapping. It was a long shot, but I could hope.

"Maybe I could make the time to help. In fact, if we're together on a case, we can talk about me and Rory, too."

Val had missed out on her childhood. Her parents were murdered, and she'd been with her sister when they found the bodies. Emma, her sister, had dragged Val to Vancouver and into a life of prostitution. Then Emma had disappeared — for the first time. That's when Val found me. We'd rescued Emma and taken down a gang of human traffickers. Now, Val sometimes acted like a kid and sometimes like an old wise woman. Today she was a kid.

I did feel bad for her, but I'm not the best person to give advice on love or commitment. To be honest, Jake's job was perfect for me. He was away on location most of the time. We never got to the point where we irritated each other into homicide.

"If you help on the case, I need you to be thinking about

that, not about Rory." I couldn't just say no — again. "Can you come tonight and help me out?"

"Like a lookout? You don't need that. You probably want me there so you can send me for coffee." She laughed and stood. "What else have you got on the go?"

"A missing person case," I said. "The searches are still running."

Val snorted. "So, you aren't too busy to talk." I guess she figured repeating that would make me see things her way.

Why hadn't I sent her on her way? She was going to get it out of me eventually, so why did I fight it? "I got a new case this morning. A favor for one of my neighbors."

"You can do a favor for a stranger, but not for me?"

She was trying to sound offended, but I knew she was just being a pain in the ass. It was how she always got what she wanted out of me.

"Not a stranger: Iain," I snapped. Knowing she was pressing my buttons and being able to control my reactions were two different things. "Someone is holding his dog for ransom."

I expected her to laugh. But she didn't. "Mickey?"

"Yeah, to be honest, I'm not sure I can help."

"You gotta. If Mickey is missing, he might be hurt. He could be lost. He's a great dog, but he's not that good at tracking and stuff."

The emotions were real, and that was something Val rarely showed. I had no idea she knew the dog.

"Iain got a ransom note," I said, keeping it to the minimum.

Now she started pacing. "What are you going to do first?"

"Don't you mean what are we going to do?" If she felt so strongly, I could use the help. Val was right about me not being that busy, but if anything came up on the missing woman, I'd have to drop the other cases to follow up. I wasn't going to just bring a woman back to her husband. I had to make sure there was no abuse going on, or any other good reason to leave.

Val slumped again, all of her energy and excitement draining out. "I'll try to make some room in my schedule. I have four new clients, and this thing with Rory." She sighed. "I can put him off." Her voice became hopeful, as if she thought that would guilt me into giving her advice.

"I can do the first bits. You figure out your business, and your love life. I'll call if I need help." That was the best I could do. Seeing Val break out of her emotional armor was enough to commit me to finding Mickey.

I could set up alerts on my other cases. I'd get a ping on my phone when results came in.

Val stepped forward and for a second, I thought she was going to hug me. Then she stepped away. I guess she hadn't made that much progress. At least she allowed Rory to touch her.

She grabbed her purse and started for the door. "Yeah, let me know when you need me on the Mickey case."

Val was gone before I answered.

FOUR

I gave up pretending I wasn't going to help Iain. It still irked that I had to stoop to dog retrieval, but Val had a point. I wasn't really busy. And I wanted to be able to face Iain when we passed each other on the street.

He'd been so upset when we talked, that I decided to call and see if he'd thought of any other information that might constitute a lead.

He was back at work, so I had to negotiate a receptionist whose job description must have contained the words brick and wall somewhere near the top of the skills list. After greeting me with all the cheerfulness of a scripted corporate front woman, she had to be convinced that I wasn't trying to get information on one of MainlineData's clients.

When I finally got Iain on the phone, he sounded like he'd gotten himself under control.

"Charity," he said. "Did something happen? Is Mickey home?"

He sounded so hopeful that I hated to answer. "No. Have you heard anything more?" If the dognappers didn't tell him how to pay the ransom soon, it wouldn't be good.

"Nothing. Did you talk to the spa? I don't want to be pushy, but what if something happens to Mickey. What if the dognappers never tell me where to meet them?"

So, he'd made the same leap. If I was going to take on the case, I couldn't sit around and wait. I needed to be proactive. "Iain, slow down a bit. First, I'll take the case. You need to sign a client agreement. Can I email it?" That was another thing Matthieu taught me. Without a signed agreement, the client could back out of the case when it got hard.

"Yeah. I'll drop off the ransom on my way home. And I'll add a grand as an advance. Is that okay?"

It was more than okay, but I wasn't going to argue. "Call the daycare when you send the signed agreement back. I'll start with them."

"It's a dog spa, Charity," Iain said. He had me wait on the line while he printed and signed the agreement. He scanned it and emailed it back and asked me to confirm receipt. It was way more formal than I'd expected, but maybe it was how he worked.

"I'll call the spa right now," he said.

"Iain, before you go. I have some questions." I needed a bit more information from him before I followed up on the people who'd let Mickey leave with strangers.

"Why? It should be easy to get answers from them."

"True, but there's nothing to say they are at fault. Whoever took Mickey was pretty convincing. And these questions are for you."

"Okay, I have a few minutes before I have to go into a meeting."

Now, all of a sudden, he was too busy to help me find Mickey? "So, has anyone been hanging around when you take Mickey out?"

There was a long pause.

"Iain, I'm trying to figure out why they took your dog and not another one."

"I take him to the dog park at the end of Cardero. I didn't notice anyone lurking."

"So, only the regulars?" It might be a dead end, but the dognappers wouldn't just take a random dog from the daycare.

"Maybe some new ones, but everyone there has a dog. There are some kids who hang out across the way, but I don't remember anything odd."

It was possible that he didn't remember, but his pauses made me think he was hiding something. Now it was getting interesting.

Maybe Mickey wasn't the target, just the tool. "Is there any reason someone would want to hurt you?"

Another pause. I was getting a bad feeling about this.

"Iain, if you don't help, I won't be able to find your dog."

A sigh. "There might be a few. I don't want to go into it unless I have to."

I wasn't expecting there to be more than one. What had my neighbor done to have as many as a few enemies? "How will you know you have to?"

"It's not the kind of thing these people would do. They wouldn't take Mickey. They'd come after me directly."

I wasn't going to run around in circles trying to find a dog that could be just a smoke screen. "Look, you don't know how people will react. You were upset enough when we talked to make me feel like you were hurt. Everything you tell me is kept confidential. I don't gossip about clients."

A longer pause this time. So long that I checked my phone to see if we'd been disconnected. "Iain?"

"I have to go. I'll come by tonight to tell you what you need to know. Just concentrate on Mickey."

He hung up before I could try to get more information. I

needed to know if the 'few people' were after the same thing, or whether Iain had a past filled with criminal behavior. I couldn't take the time to research him before I headed out. It was getting late in the day and I needed to follow up on Mickey and other cases.

I called back and left a message on Iain's voicemail, telling him that if he wasn't at my place by nine, he'd have to come back tomorrow. He didn't need to know that I was going to be on another case. I liked my clients to think they were the only priority. The truth was they were; at the time I was working on them.

I stuffed my laptop into my bag along with a blank file that I could start for Iain. I flipped open Sara Lyman's thin file. Her picture was clipped to the left side. She was one of those people who blended in. In this photo, she was wearing a blue sweater and jeans. She had blond hair cut in a short bob, and a nice smile. Someone you'd see on the sideline of the soccer field cheering on a kid. Someone you'd pass in the mall without noticing. She would be hard to find if I couldn't get a solid lead.

My first stop was the dog daycare — I refused to call it a dog spa — and then Sara's employer. If I was really lucky, she had a best friend there who could shine some light on why she'd left her husband, and where she might have gone.

FIVE

I spent the walk to my car, which was parked at The Bayshore, trying to understand why someone who kidnapped dogs would take so long to send the ransom instructions. Were they amateurs, or really experienced? It was sometimes hard to tell the difference. Amateurs could look like they were doing everything right, but it was all by accident. Professionals would have everything down to a fine art, and still things would go wrong. Maybe waiting for instructions made people more invested in paying up.

I waved at the cashier as I passed into the gloom of the parking lot. My phone rang, the noise bouncing off the concrete walls. This time I looked at the caller ID: Lu.

"Hey! What's up?" I didn't have Bluetooth in my car, so I stepped back into the sunlight to take her call.

"I'm Bridezillaing again," she said. Her voice was all tight and tensed up. Lu was usually my calming influence.

"I'm heading out for some interviews. Do you want to meet for coffee?" If she was downtown, I could squeeze her in between the daycare and the office.

"No. I just need your advice," she said. "I'm going crazy."

This didn't sound good. Planning a wedding was stressful — I have no experience in doing it, but I've seen a lot of the blow ups that can happen. "You've done this before. Isn't it easier the second time around?"

She laughed; it was not a happy sound. "Last time it was done by a planner. The mothers took control and we just followed orders. This time no mothers, no planner, and we're from different cultures."

I still didn't see the problem. "What does Matthieu want?"

"I haven't a clue. He says he doesn't care. That his first marriage was a civil ceremony. That it's whatever I want."

That sounded reasonable to me, but I knew from experience with Jake, that sometimes there were lines to read between and sometimes there weren't. It was tricky to know for sure when the lines were really there or were only in your own head.

"So, what if he's telling you the truth? What do you want?"

"Today I'm all for not getting married at all. It was easier before we decided to make it formal. I know Matthieu usually says what he means, but I see him looking at churches, and he comments on how pretty brides look when we pass someone posing for their pictures. It's that time of year."

Yes, Vancouver had a season. In late spring through late fall, you'd wander by wedding parties in Stanley Park, or Queen Elizabeth, or Lynn Canyon. The backdrops of rose gardens and waterfalls were prized. I figure if Jake and I ever decide to do the deed, we'd find a different site for pictures. Maybe under the Burrard Bridge: graffiti, drifting litter, and all.

"If it was up to you?" I reminded her of the question. "And not getting married isn't an option. What would you do?"

"Vegas."

I couldn't think of any argument against it. "Just tell me when to book the ticket."

"I wish. It's not really up to me. There are aunts and cousins on my side who would have a heart attack if I ran away to get married. They're not exactly happy about the fact that Matthieu isn't Chinese."

"I don't know what to tell you, Lu." I checked my watch and tried not to sound impatient. If I didn't head out soon, I'd be stuck in the first wave of rush hour. "You should talk to Matthieu and figure it out."

"I can't do that again."

The tension had crept back into her voice. "Okay, then the best that I can do is to say that Matthieu will be happy with whatever makes you happy. I need to go. Can we try to get together in a couple of days?"

"If you aren't going to help me stop freaking out, then I guess we don't need to talk."

That wasn't Lu at all. She was right about the Bridezilla attack.

"I want to help, Lu, but I have to work."

"Fine," she said, then ended the call.

Great! When did I become the peacemaker? Where did I suddenly come up with love advice. First Val and now Lu. It was probably better to let her cool down before I tried again. I slipped my phone into my bag and headed into the parking lot.

If I got what I needed at the stakeout tonight, I'd make sure Lu and I had a night of dinner and drinking that would make her let go of the freak out. And I couldn't ignore the relief at having more than one case to keep me from helping her; relief and a heavy weight of cowardice.

I checked the address again for Dog Heaven — a really unfortunate name — it was about a ten-minute walk. And Sara's workplace was downtown. Now that the traffic was building up, it made more sense to go on foot. It would give me time to find a wedding planner for Lu. Maybe a professional would be able to get them to agree on a plan. I sure didn't want to get between my best friend and my new business partner.

SIX

I got to Dog Heaven and had to wait for the owner to finish grooming a standard poodle before she would talk to me. The poodle looked like a topiary after she was done, but the dog didn't seem to mind.

"Yeah, Iain called," the woman said before introducing herself. "Mickey was a good dog."

I pulled out a card and handed it to her. "I'm Charity Deacon. Iain didn't tell me your name." I wasn't going to let her keep going without the niceties. When people gave you their name, it made them obligated to you in a small way. Sometimes that was just enough for them to give you information you didn't ask for. Like they were more helpful after the introductions and more engaged with sorting out a problem.

"Oh, Gwen. Sorry, I spend most of my time with dogs. They like to sniff at you for identification."

I didn't envy her. Even this short time in the room with ten dogs was giving me a headache. "So, did you see anything suspicious before Mickey went missing?"

She scowled. "Not missing. Taken. I hate people who do

this kind of thing. I know they are only dogs, but for some of my clients, the dog is all they have."

I nodded as if I agreed with her. "Was there anyone hanging around?" I repeated the question. Perhaps her association with the canines had shortened her attention span.

"No. We don't really watch for that kind of thing. I mean, it's not unusual for people to want to pet the dogs. We get kids coming up all the time."

This wasn't going anywhere, so I had to go for the hard question. It was a risk that she'd clam up, but since Gwen hadn't given me any information, it wasn't that much of a risk. "So, what made you trust the guy who picked up Mickey?" There I did my best not to come across as blaming her.

Gwen reached into a bowl of bone shaped cookies and held up her handful. All ten dogs stood on their hind legs. It was a little disturbing, like they were hers to command in the coming apocalypse.

After tossing each dog a treat, she turned her attention back to me. "I told Iain this. I'd seen the guy talking to Iain a couple of times on the street outside. I thought they were related like the guy said."

Iain hadn't mentioned that to me. In fairness, I hadn't actually asked him what he'd done to find Mickey.

I made a note. "What did the guy look like?"

"Okay, so this isn't much. I see a lot of people, but like I said, I'd seen him with Iain. So, he was skinny, his hair was cut real short, like a soldier or something. It was black, but, you know, dyed. He was kind of jumpy. I thought at the time he was just nervous about the dogs, but now I think maybe he was tweaking." She took a deep breath and I realized she'd been holding in a lot of emotion with the information. If you asked me, it was guilt. And it was deserved.

"That helps," I said. "Is there anything else that might help me find Mickey?"

"If the chip isn't working, then no, I don't have a clue."

"What chip?" If Iain had kept something else from me, I was going to dump the case. Oh, who was I kidding. I might not be a dog person, but Mickey didn't deserve to be kidnapped.

"There's a chip under his skin. Iain has an app that tells him where Mickey is," she said it as if it was common knowledge.

"Thanks." I tried to keep the annoyance out of my voice, but it didn't work.

"I told Iain to check the chip when he called. I guess he forgot about it. Lots of my clients do. Unless the dog is a runner, they don't have to use it."

Yeah, forgot.

"Thanks, that's a lot of help," I said. I dropped my notebook in my bag. "I'll call him."

"Let me know what happens, okay? I like Mickey."

Perhaps I was reading between the lines, but she didn't say anything about liking Iain.

Outside, I called Iain. He answered right away.

"You have a locator app?" I asked, not willing to waste any more time with him.

Iain paused; I was getting used to that. "It's not working."

Of course. "Is there any other way to check?"

"I've been in meetings all afternoon. I haven't had time to call the vet. He has the information."

Defensive.

"Where's the vet?"

Iain gave me the address. It was only a few blocks away. I checked my watch. I had just enough time to check on Mickey's chip and still get to Sara's workplace before end of business. "Call them. I'll go over now."

Iain agreed. I hung up. He didn't seem too broken up about

Mickey now. Maybe he could separate work and home life better than most people, but I think a day off to find his missing pet wouldn't be out of the question. My gut was telling me there was something off about the whole situation, but Mickey shouldn't suffer because his owner was weird.

SEVEN

In less than five minutes, I was sitting in the vet's waiting room. It wasn't unusual that a case would be more about waiting than about doing stuff, but it didn't mean I liked it. Vet waiting rooms are different from offices. If you aren't all that comfortable around animals, it would be a horrible experience. There were three other people in the room. A woman with her dog in a large purse. It was one of those hairy ones that vibrated with energy, or nerves. Its hair fluttering with the trembling of its body. A cat was giving a growly whine and trying to push itself through a hole in the travel case. It was going for the eye-first route. The third pet was in a glass bowl with a lid. The kid holding it kept tapping the side. I tried not to look; I really did. Inside was a large hairy spider. What kind of pet was that?

The worse thing was my nagging conscience. Every minute I spent on this was a minute I couldn't spend on a missing person — human person. It's not that I hate dogs, but people are more important to me. And sitting here meant I'd have to get take-out for tonight instead of getting home in time to eat before I headed out on surveillance. Okay, going home to eat still meant take out, but my irritation lumped it in with the list of things I hated about waiting.

"Ms. Deacon?" a warm male voice interrupted my grump.

I looked up to see a man in his sixties. Nice eyes, nice smile, nothing that made him stand out. If I were casting a movie that needed a nice old veterinarian, he'd fit the bill. "Dr. Lawson?"

"That's me. Mickey's owner called. I understand that you need to know where he is." He waited for me to nod before adding, "Come on into my office. It should only take a minute or two."

When we got into his office, Dr. Lawson started pulling drawers open and sorting through the contents. After a minute, I asked, "Can I help?"

He looked up and gave me a sheepish smile. "I'm looking for the passwords."

"You don't have them memorized?" I tried to keep the groan out of my voice.

"I did, but then the system changed, and I had to have one of those stupid long passwords with all kinds of numbers and symbols. I couldn't figure out a way to make sense of it, so I wrote it down and put it in a safe place."

"So safe, that you can't remember where?" I laughed to make him feel like I sympathized.

"Yes, exactly." He kept opening drawers. There were a lot of them in the room. Four on his desk and then he had one of those antique apothecary cabinets. The ones with tiny sections that were supposed to hold things like nightshade and eye of newt.

"When did you last use it?" Maybe it would jog his memory.

He didn't take his attention away from his search. "A month ago, maybe more."

"So, dogs don't get lost?"

He chuckled. "Not as often as you think, and most people

use the app. I don't know why Mr. O'Keith doesn't. It's very reliable."

He turned to look at me. "How much do you know about him?"

It was a weird question coming from a vet, but you never know where you'll get a clue that solves the case, so I answered. "I don't know him that well, but he does seem a little distracted."

"I suppose he's very busy." Dr. Lawson kept looking through drawers as he continued. "I get the feeling that he needs Mickey to keep him grounded. That his job is stressful."

So, no information, maybe he just liked to gossip. "I don't know about that. You said the app is reliable, how many people have it?"

He turned and smiled. "This particular version is new. I have about ten of my patients using it. Mr. O'Keith was excited to be part of the test."

"Have any of the others stopped working?" I wondered if this tracker thing was going to be worthwhile.

"There's two parts to it. The... beacon, I suppose you'd call it, is implanted in the animal's shoulder. It runs on a battery like a pacemaker. It has never malfunctioned as far as I know. There are other vets on the test program, so they have a lot of data." He'd stopped searching while he talked. "The other part is the app on the owner's phone. I don't know if that's as reliable."

So, Iain could be telling the truth. "Oh, well. If it worked all the time, I wouldn't have a client."

"Ah!" Dr. Lawson pushed a drawer closed and held up a tiny Moleskine. "Here they are." He checked the label on the drawer. "Rosemary. For remembrance. I guess I had a system."

I refrained from comment. If I didn't engage in the small talk, maybe I'd be out of here in a minute.

He reached below his desk and I heard the sound of a fan turn on and the grinding clunk of an old computer starting up.

"It will take a minute or two to get online," he said in a way that made me certain we were going to deal with dial-up.

Fortunately, he was in the twenty-first century with his internet provider. He typed in the code and a map popped onto the screen. There were fifty flags at least.

"Which one is Mickey?"

He looked at me like I was the one who didn't know her password and used a ten-year-old desktop computer.

"They are all Mickey. I put in his ID number. But this is over the last week. Give it time to sync with the chip and we'll get his current location."

As he spoke, the flags faded out, one at a time until there was only one left. Then that blinked off. Dr. Lawson brought down a menu and chose details. There was a list of addresses and cross streets and what looked like longitude and latitude numbers.

"The chip has been deactivated," he finally said. "Look the list shows him somewhere on the North Shore, probably on Grouse. Then it goes out. Why would someone deactivate it?"

He looked at me as if I had the answers. Well, this time I was pretty sure I did have them. "He was dognapped. I guess they found the chip."

Dr. Lawson's face turned red. "If they've hurt Mickey..."

I was pretty sure they'd hurt the dog because I couldn't imagine a dognapper being a dog lover. I hoped they hadn't killed him. "Tell me how this works." I wanted to be very sure I was following up on a good lead.

"The chip sends out a signal, a ping they call it, every few minutes. It stops working if it's removed. Maybe they just cut it out. Mickey would be fine. It's just under his skin."

"So, when they took it out," I said, looking at the list, "it would show exactly where they were?"

Dr. Lawson printed the list. "If my memory serves, they had him going in circles in the last while. It won't show his exact location anyway."

He brought up another map on his computer and started typing in the locations. I watched as each entry appeared on the map and zoomed it closer in so we could see exactly where Mickey had been.

The Grouse Grind.

Dr. Lawson laughed at my groan. "Don't worry. He's not on the Grind. If he were, the markers would show him going up. My guess is they took him to a trail nearby because the Grind is too busy to hide a dog from observation."

"Can I have the printout?" I could only hope that the dognappers had simply taken him somewhere quiet where they wouldn't be observed and not deep into the woods.

"Of course." He handed me the list. "Bring Mickey here when you find him. I'll check him out. We don't want him going back to Iain with ticks or worse. I'll call you if he moves."

I promised and then stuffed the paper into my bag. I'd be better off waiting for rush hour to be over than going now. Arriving at the foot of the Grind after steaming in traffic wasn't going to make me the best dog hunter. Besides, Val might be willing to join me. With luck, we'd have Mickey back home before I had to go on stakeout.

EIGHT

There was still time to visit TZM Consulting, Sara's workplace, before heading back to get my car.

This time it wasn't as easy as asking to talk to the boss. In Sara's workplace, I needed someone who knew her well enough to have information on her personal life. Her husband swore they had no problems, but it wasn't smart detective work to just believe him. It didn't help his case that he had no idea who her friends were. In my experience, everyone had one friend at least. One person they could talk to about their inner fears and plans. If Sara didn't want her husband to know who that was, then she was hiding a big fat dirty secret.

The receptionist said that she was new and didn't know anyone beyond their name and telephone extension, so she called Sara's boss to meet me.

When she arrived in the waiting area, Mae Wilkins looked harried and impatient. She was taller than me, pretty unusual. She was skinny the way people who smoked too much and ate too little got; unhealthy, but not sick.

"Hi, come up to my office and we'll see what I can do to help you." She started walking away, assuming I'd follow and continued talking without looking at me. "I didn't know Sara all that well, we're not a close group. It happens in consulting firms." She glanced back from the top of the stairs; making sure I was keeping up, I guess. "Teams work together, but not all the time."

I nodded. At least now I knew what the company did. "What kind of consulting did Sara do?"

We were in an open area filled with clustered workstations. A few people filled one of the pods, all bent over the keyboard like they were watching a typing lesson. Mae didn't answer. Suddenly she seemed aware that the information she had might be confidential.

She pointed to a glass-walled room in the corner. "That's my office. Do you want coffee?"

I shook my head; I needed to make this fast.

When we were sitting across the desk from one another, Mae started talking again. "She worked primarily with MainlineData. They are also a consulting firm."

Coincidence?

"Yes," I said. "Data security, I think." If there was a connection between Iain and Sara, I'd better find out now. "Are they a large company? If I talked to someone over there, would they likely know her?"

Mae sat straighter in her chair. I got the feeling I'd triggered some kind of defense mechanism. "I can't give you any information on clients."

I leaned forward, trying to project calm professionalism. "Of course. I have my own connections there. I was just wondering if maybe Sara had a friend there."

Mae relaxed a little. "I don't think so. Sara was a private person. She didn't attend any of our little social events. We try to create a team atmosphere, but as I said, most of our people don't work consistently together."

It was like Sara had built a life for herself that she could just leave when she felt like it. The husband might just have been window dressing. There were only a few places she could be that I couldn't penetrate: witness protection of some sort, or a government spy agency. I'd find her eventually if she simply wanted out of her life, or some corporation wanted her knowledge — or if she was dead.

"So, there was no one here who would know why she would leave?" Sometimes people get tired of answering no to the same question and try to vary their answer. And sometimes that was all I needed.

Mae glanced over my shoulder, then down at her hands. She was getting ready to tell me something, but she didn't want to get caught doing it.

In normal circumstances, I would have waited her out, but I wanted to close Mickey's case before I went on surveillance. So, I pushed a little harder than usual. "I won't spill any secrets, Mae. I need my reputation for discretion."

She inspected her nails for a few more seconds. Then she straightened her jacket. "Not exactly a friend. You know that every office has certain types of employees, right?"

I nodded. "Yeah, there's always someone who wants to take on the social stuff, someone who parties a little too hard, someone who knows way too much about everyone's business."

"Zane Tomkins." She relaxed as soon as the name was out. "His job is to coordinate all of the client assignments, advise on the best paring of consultant to client. We knew he was a gossip, but we don't use that title. He has a knack of getting to the information we need to be successful. It is an asset in his job, but he doesn't seem to understand the meaning of the word boundaries. If anyone knows anything about Sara, it will be Zane."

I didn't care about his job performance. "Can I talk to him?"

"You have to be discreet," Mae said. "Not just with the information you get, but also with what I just told you."

I figured Zane knew exactly what they thought of him, but I agreed to her request. "I'll sign an agreement if you need me to."

Mae laughed. "Oh yes, a piece of paper that Zane can get hold of. Your word works for me; a signature doesn't mean anything if your word isn't good. I'll get him in here. Is it okay for me to tell him why?"

"Just say I'm looking into Sara's disappearance."

She left me alone in the office while she found Zane. I was tempted to go looking through the files on her desk, but I needed her to trust me, and everyone would see me doing it. Damn glass walls.

I turned around to see what was going on outside. It was a little after normal work hours, but there were still a few heads bent over keyboards. Mae was coming back to the office. She didn't have anyone with her. I guess Zane was one of the people who kept regular hours.

"He's getting coffee," she said. "I can send him in. How long do you think this is going to take?"

I had to make it quick. "If he tells me what he knows, probably less than five minutes. But that's unusual. I only have a half hour anyway. Will that work?"

She nodded. "I'll lock up my files, and let you use the room. Come find me in the break room before you go. I have to let you out."

And she'd want to know what I learned; I was sure.

She locked the files in a drawer and grabbed her purse and jacket. There was no way I could slip out without her, so it was going to be harder for me to dodge questions.

NINE

"Hi," a male voice interrupted us. "You wanted to talk to me."

"Zane, this is Charity Deacon. She has some questions about Sara," Mae did the introductions as she walked past him to the door.

Zane was dressed in what must be business casual for TZM; dark pants, loafers, and a white shirt, no tie. I stood to shake hands, and he only came up to my shoulder. That put him at around five four. Blond, well-groomed and just a little pudgy.

I held out my hand. "Good to meet you, Zane. I just have a couple of questions."

His shake was firm and efficient. The kind of handshake they teach you in Toastmasters. "I'm always happy to help in any way I can."

He sat on the other client chair and folded his hands in his lap, eyes on me expectantly. I pulled out my notebook. "You probably want to get home, so I'll get to the point. I've been hired by Sara's husband to find her, and I can't seem to get any traction. I'm hoping you have some information that I can use."

He raised his eyebrows. "Why me?"

Like he didn't know.

"It seems you were the closest she had to a friend." I smiled and looked directly at him. Then I leaned in and added, "You may have information that other people, people she didn't like so much, wouldn't know."

My answer seemed to please him, because he smiled and leaned forward mimicking my pose. He was good, but I knew it was all an act. He knew how to connect with someone just well enough to get the tidbits of information that they'd prefer to keep quiet.

"I mostly just did the scheduling," Zane said. "She wasn't interested in having friends. I always assumed her personal life was full enough." He leaned away.

I couldn't get rid of the feeling he was holding something back. He thought this was a game. Maybe an appeal to his protective side would work. "I know it's not polite to talk about a friend, but please tell me whatever you know. I need to find her and make sure she's safe. Who knows what's happening to her right now."

"Maybe I don't know anything," he said it with a smile on his lips. "What if she's better off staying lost? I mean, maybe she had a reason."

He definitely knew something. I just hadn't found the right hook yet to get him to spill.

"I have a lot of experience in this kind of thing," I lied. "I'm pretty sure that there's no reason for Sara to hide from her husband. Am I wrong?"

"What happens if you are, wrong I mean?"

This was painful. Despite his display of caution, I was sure Zane just wanted to feel important. "What I do know is that if I don't, at minimum, let her husband know she's safe, he'll keep looking. Is that a good idea?"

He sat back. Maybe I'd given him a new perspective on his

information. Maybe he did care more about Sara than about gossip.

"Fair enough. I've only seen them together at company parties. He's a tradesman or something, right?" He left it there as though we both agreed that people who worked with their hands were less important, or inherently untrustworthy.

"Perhaps you don't know anything, then," I said, reaching for my bag to put away the notebook.

Zane leaned in again. "Ask your questions."

I thought he was better at the game than that. All it took was a threat to his self-image as the office gossip and he was hooked. I started at the beginning, keeping the satisfaction I felt at his capitulation out of my voice. "What about her marriage?"

"Like I said, I only actually met her husband at the company picnic. We do an event every season, but he'd never come before. I heard he was supposed to be a big shot in entertainment. Something went wrong, and now he's a plumber."

"Did Sara seem okay with that?" It must have been a shock to find out your potentially famous husband turned out to be just a regular guy.

"She never said." He smirked. "If I had to guess, I'd say she was biding her time until she could find a better option."

That was new information. If Sara's husband suspected that she was looking around, would he pay the bill? Another problem for another day.

"Do you think he knew that?"

Zane snorted a laugh. "He wasn't that perceptive."

"Did she strike you as someone who'd just leave?"

Zane sat back in the chair. "Who knows." He checked his watch. "I should head out now. Unless you have other questions."

I'd hit the bottom of his information. He didn't even have a crumb to build a story on. And he'd just realized I wasn't going to hand over any gossip. Zane was done with me and Sara.

TEN

I stood outside the offices of TZM Consulting thinking about my next step. The traffic was lighter, but rush hour wasn't over by a long shot. I would have to deal with the slow traffic now because I didn't want to let Mickey sit any longer waiting for rescue — if that's what he needed.

I wanted backup on the trail because I wasn't an outdoors kind of girl. Wandering around the local mountains wasn't my idea of a good time. If I had someone to go with me, then maybe I wouldn't get lost, or eaten by a bear, or fall off the edge of the trail.

I called Val.

Her phone went directly to voicemail. No rings, nothing. Her phone was off, or she was out of the service area. I left a message to call me back ASAP so we could go to the North Shore. I called Dr. Lawson while I waited for her to respond.

"There's no change. I hope he's okay," Dr. Lawson said.

How far could the dog go without the app noticing? "I'm sure he's just sitting there waiting for someone to pick him up," I said. "I'll be at his location within the hour."

"I'm on my way home now. Call me when you find him, and I'll open the office."

I agreed, and we ended the call.

So far nothing from Val. If I didn't hear from her by the time I got back to the car, I was on my own. I entered the location information into my map program and it zoomed in and out before sticking a pin in the spot where I should find Mickey. Not far from the parking lot at the bottom of the Grind.

Time to call Iain again.

"Charity, how did it go at the vet's?" He was eager for news again. This guy was making me question my instincts about people. One minute he's nonchalant about the situation, the next he's worried and desperate for Mickey's rescue.

I didn't want to make any promises. "I have a lead. I might have something to report soon. How long will you be at work?"

"I can work late. It's probably better for me to stay here, right? In case you need me."

It didn't matter to me where he was. As long as he didn't come with me to find the dog. I had nothing to show whether Mickey was alive or dead. And I didn't want to have to deal with Iain's reaction in the middle of the woods if we found a body. "Actually I have a question for you."

"Anything that will help you find Mickey."

"Funny coincidence, it's about another case." If Iain could point me in the right direction, I'd save time on finding out who Sara worked with. "Did you ever meet, or work with, Sara Lyman?"

Another of his pauses; at least this time it probably meant he was thinking about my question. "The name isn't familiar," he said, finally.

I was getting used to reading the subtext in Iain's voice. This time there was something unsaid between the words. "Do you think you can ask around, discretely, of course."

"I'm busy, Charity," he said almost before I finished. "And I need you to find Mickey."

"I'm on the case Iain," I said. So, he didn't want to ask. If I was right, and he was lying, maybe Sara was having an affair with someone higher on the corporate ladder than Iain. He didn't strike me as enough of a step up from her husband for Sara to bother.

Iain gave a short sigh, his impatience spilling through the phone. "Fine. If she worked with us, HR would have some information. Do you want me to find out?"

"No, it's not urgent. I'll call you soon." I closed the call.

I'd make the inquiry, just to make sure I got the right information by asking the right questions. That department usually took privacy a little too seriously for a PI to get help without some finesse. I'd have to do some thinking on my next step. Maybe her credit card records would be ready by the time I got back.

I picked up a taco at a truck a block away from my car. Still no contact with Val.

Reluctant to go alone, I drove around the block and headed toward Val's apartment. It would only add ten minutes to my drive and even she would find it hard to say no to me in person.

ELEVEN

Val's current apartment was in an old house in the West End. It was a basement studio and would have normally been out of her price range. But Val was resourceful. She'd done an organization job for the building owner and negotiated a huge break on the rent for a year. It would be too small for her and Rory. I had no idea where they would be living, if they moved in together.

My phone rang as soon as I found a parking spot a block away from her home.

"Hey." Val spoke before I could get my usual greeting out.

"Did you get my message?"

"Yeah. Look I can't come over to the North Shore right now."

I wasn't surprised, but I also wasn't going to give up that easily. "Are you home?"

"Yeah," she said. Then more cautiously, "Why?"

I put on my cheerful voice. "I'm in the neighborhood. Why don't I come by? Maybe I can help you so you can help me."

I was at her basement door before she could come up with an excuse. I knocked and said into the phone, "Come on, Val. Let me in."

"Fine!" It was said with the world-weariness of a teenager. Val might be a successful businesswoman, but she still hadn't hit twenty.

The door opened and I stepped into the gloomy entrance. "I thought you'd be packing."

"We're still talking about it. I got a good deal here for another couple of months. If Rory didn't have all that video equipment, we could live here; like a test run."

Cold feet; something I could relate to when it came to committing. "But he has all that stuff. Where are you talking about moving to?"

"We haven't got that far. I just got him to believe me when I said I wasn't going to move into his folk's pool house. No matter how cool his dad might be, I don't want that. You want a Coke or something?"

Rory's dad was a high-profile criminal lawyer. He was cool by the country club standard, but not even close by Val's. "No, I'm good. If you aren't packing why won't you come help me?"

"Jeez why is it all about you?"

My light and breezy act wasn't going anywhere. Val was mad about something, and she wasn't going to tell me what it was. I just hoped it wasn't at me. "It's not, but Mickey is on the side of Grouse Mountain and I'd like a bit of help in locating him — before a bear gets him."

She sighed. "He's a dog. Don't you just whistle?"

"I only took this case because you shamed me into it. Look it'll only be an hour — two at most. Then we're home and the job's done. I can get back to my real cases." I also didn't want to admit to grouchy Val that I was anxious about being alone on a trail.

"I've been on jobs with you before. I seem to remember that you are bad at estimating time." She slumped on a beanbag chair. "You know it could take forever. Do you have a headlamp, in case it gets dark before you find him?"

"Yes." I didn't want a repeat of the time in Squamish when I had to trek down the side of mountain in the dark. "I have a headlamp, and water. What I need is someone with me."

"Rory is coming over later for dinner." She pointed to the small table set up with plates and cutlery. "Your boyfriend might prefer to be on the other side of the world, but mine is right here."

That hurt more than I expected. Given the state that a simple decision was putting Val in, I should be happy Jake and I weren't rubbing each other's nerves every day. But Val's comment just made me miss Jake.

"You think having Rory here means you can play with his life?" The words were out before I could stop them. "Relationships are about compromise, Val."

"How would you know?" she asked.

I'm normally a pretty patient person. It's critical for a PI to be willing to wait for the case to develop. Val had this ability to make me want to spit fire. Maybe it was just the teenage attitude, when I knew she could be an adult. Maybe it was my fear of getting lost in the woods. But I'd had enough, and I was only a few heartbeats away from saying something that she might not recover from.

I took a breath and then said, "Fine, you stay here. I'll go by myself. I don't need your help. I don't know why I thought you might be interested." It sounded calm and rational in my head, but it came out as petulant as Val was being.

"Okay, then I guess you should get started." Val rolled her eyes.

I turned and left. I deliberately didn't slam her door.

TWELVE

I got lucky; there was no accident on the bridge, so here I was twenty-five minutes after I left Val, standing in the parking lot at the Grouse Grind. At least it wasn't raining, in fact it was still light out, that gentle light just before dusk. Also the time for gnats and other nasty bugs to come out.

Only one other car had pulled in with me and the people inside had walked toward the trail head without looking around. I guess it was getting a bit late to start the Grind. I hoped they were experienced and could do the trek up to the top within an hour. Unless they were really fit, they'd find themselves in a bit of trouble about halfway up. People who knew the path, and were in shape, could finish it in just about an hour, most people could take two, or more.

They weren't my problem. I pulled out my phone and looked for a signal. It was strong. Checking the map, I saw that Mickey should be about a hundred meters up and off to the side of the main path. I zoomed and the site was labeled. The junction of the Baden Powell Trail. I guess I was doing a bit of the Grind, but I was going to walk down when I had the dog, not up. Screw the one-way only rules. It was just the start anyway. I'd be careful not to damage the trail.

I dropped a bottle of water in my bag. Climbing was thirsty work. On second thoughts, I added a second bottle for Mickey and a bag of beef jerky just in case the dognappers hadn't fed him.

The little flag hadn't moved. If Mickey was tied up, it might be a problem. Not wildlife; the path was too busy for animals to roam during the day. But I had to be able to release him. I made sure I had a multi-tool in my bag. It would have to do.

I sent a text to Val: *On my way up, if I don't return, maybe you'll find time to let someone know where my body is.*

Yeah, I know, I should be more of an adult, but I couldn't help myself. My camera case was tucked into the corner of my car trunk. I would need it later, and there was no chance for me to get home and change before my next job. It was way too heavy to take with me. I locked the car, faced the trail, and started the walk, my phone in hand.

After ten minutes I learned how out of shape I was. Panting and sweating on the least steep part of the climb didn't bode well if I had to hunt for Mickey on the Baden Powell. The junction was clearly marked, and I was happy to see that the climb was much less steep.

I kept zooming the app and turning around to make sure I was still on the right track. The distance on the phone and the actual walk were a little skewed — or maybe that was just my mind. When it was clear that I was within feet of Mickey's location, I stepped off the trail and into the trees.

Mickey should be barking or something. Maybe they drugged him to keep him docile. It wasn't reassuring. I had no way of pulling a dog out of the forest and down a trail; at least, not one the size of Mickey. Why couldn't Iain do the same thing as every other downtown dog owner, have a purse dog?

The app wasn't changing, and I took that as a good sign. It must be working. I checked the signal strength and it was good enough, not full, but the bars were stable.

The dog had to be nearby. There wasn't much light when I got off the trail; not dark enough for the headlamp, but not far off. Maybe he was blending in. Especially if he was sleeping, he'd be down at the bottom of wherever they'd tied him to.

I had enough battery power to use the flashlight app, so I found a firm place to stand, there weren't many, and I shone the light onto the floor of the forest. Not much undergrowth with the old trees, but a lot of droppings, pinecones, and dead branches.

In the second pass, I saw something glint. Turning off the light, I kept my eyes on the spot. It might be a trail biker's power bar wrapper, but it definitely wasn't a dog.

I bent down as I got closer, and a cloud of flies rose. The shine had come from one of the studs on Mickey's collar. The flies came from a chunk of flesh.

I stumbled back. It's not like I'm a stranger to dead bodies, and I'd half expected to find a dead Mickey, but I wasn't expecting to find a piece of Mickey.

When I got myself under control, and I was sure I wasn't going to upchuck the taco, I went back to the collar. I dug around in my bag to find something to put the two clues in — I had to think of them as clues. The only thing I had was a pair of latex gloves. Oh, well, they'd work. I pulled on one of the gloves and used that hand to put the collar into the other glove. Then I grabbed the marble-sized gob of dog fur and flesh and took the glove off around it.

There was something in the chunk, a pellet of some kind. I closed my eyes and took a deep breath. I was tired, hot, cranky, and now I was going to have to dig around in this piece of Mickey to see what was there.

At least there was no body. Whoever brought him here, it was to lead me or Iain to this spot. Mickey was probably okay. They wouldn't have taken him somewhere else to kill him when there was a nice remote forest to do it. There was no blood, so they hadn't killed him here and tossed the body. It didn't make sense to drop the tracker and then kill the dog anyway.

I got a grip on my nausea, opened my eyes, and squeezed the hunk of meat until I felt something pop out. Then I peeled back the glove enough to see a little chip. As suspected, the dognappers knew enough to get rid of a locating device. All I could hope was that they knew enough dog first aid to make sure Mickey survived.

There was nothing more to keep me on the trail, so I headed back. At the junction with the Grouse Grind, I stopped and listened carefully. It was late enough that anyone starting now, would be a true fanatic. If I ran into them, I'd get a lecture, at the least. I didn't hear any huffing and puffing, so I took a peek; no one was there. I picked my way down to the parking lot. Got into my car and called Iain.

I got his voicemail. Maybe he was talking to the people who took his dog about delivering the ransom.

THIRTEEN

I had too many things going on. I could put off showing up at the warehouse for another couple of hours, but after that I needed to drop Iain's case for the day. What I couldn't do is drive around in circles calling Mickey's name. I had to get more information. If Matthieu was around, maybe he'd go see if Iain was home and if anything had changed since we last spoke. I called him from the parking lot.

"Charity," he said.

"Hey. I know you are off, but I need a big favor. Where are you?"

"It's nice to hear from you too, how are you?"

Okay, maybe I jumped into the favor too quickly. Matthieu never really caught onto the fact that I was all business when I'm on a case. Not that I couldn't take a minute to schmooze a possible lead, but as he kept reminding me, I also needed to schmooze other people so I could grow the business. "Sorry, how rude of me. How is the wedding planning going?"

He was silent for a moment. Hadn't I been nice?

"Not well, but that is the subject of a longer conversation. How are the cases coming?"

His past as a gendarme in France surfaced every once in a while, too. The practice of keeping each other up to date was a good one. I just couldn't always remember to do it. I told him about the cases he'd left, and added, "I got a new one this morning. It's more helping out a neighbor than a case, but it's urgent."

"This is the one you need me to do you a favor for?"

"It's a missing dog. You know Iain?"

"He is the one who lives on the end of the dock? The one that I'm sure has a secret?"

"Yes."

Matthieu's instincts were good. I'd never thought anything about Iain until this case. Now I agreed with Matthieu, that there was something off about Mickey's owner. "Someone took his dog and wants a ransom."

"Ah, and you have volunteered us to find Mickey?"

"It's a dog, Matthieu."

He sighed. "What is the favor?"

"Where are you?"

"I am at your house. I needed something from the safe."

So, luck wasn't running against me all the time. "I can't get in touch with Iain, so I need you to go knock on his door. Find out what's going on."

"Are you driving?"

I didn't want to leave the parking lot until I had an idea where to go. "No. I can wait here. I have to take something to a vet later." I told him what I'd found.

"Perhaps the kidnappers are experienced, and Mickey will be safe. I'll go now. Don't hang up. If he is home, you can speak to him."

I heard the door open and then Matthieu said, "He has left you a note on your door."

"Can you check to see if he's home?" I didn't like the fact that he was avoiding me. Ever since I'd agreed to help, things had gone weird. Iain, who was supposed to be worried about his dog, seemed to be doing everything he could to hinder me. My easy missing woman case was like looking for a ghost, and I was getting pissed.

I heard Matthieu knock a few times on Iain's door. Then, "It seems like no one is going to answer. But I am sure there is someone inside."

"What does the note say?" I couldn't decide if I wanted it to give me a lead or tell me he'd found his dog.

"It seems that Iain received a call from the kidnappers. They have a meeting arranged to exchange the ransom for Mickey. He is to meet them in about an hour. I do not like that he has gone alone, Charity."

There was nothing about it that I liked. "Does it say where?"

Matthieu gave me a location in East Van. It was on my way to the warehouse job. "I'll go looking, now. I'm sure it will be okay." I don't know why I lied to Matthieu, but I didn't want him tagging along. He was supposed to be on vacation.

"Be careful," he said. "Perhaps you should call Val. It wouldn't hurt to have some company."

I couldn't agree more, but I also didn't have the time or energy for another spat with Val. "She's busy. It's fine."

"What about your other cases? If you need me to, I can come back and work them." His voice carried hope that I'd say yes.

I wasn't going to get between Lu and Matthieu.

"The wedding won't plan itself." I started the car, and plugged in my earbud— I know, it's not Bluetooth, but it worked well enough. I might as well head to East Van while we talked, it felt efficient.

FOURTEEN

"Perhaps you can do me a favor in return," Matthieu said.

I knew he wouldn't ask for something unless it was important, and it couldn't wait until I'd done the Mickey thing. That didn't stop me from worrying about the change; Matthieu had never asked me for a favor. He was always on top of any situation. Cop training came in handy for our jobs, but all of that made it impossible to deny him. "Whatever I can do."

He paused. I let him think through what he was going to ask as I pulled onto the Lion's Gate bridge. It couldn't be that bad, right?

"I would not normally ask you for advice about this subject, but I am at a standstill."

My stomach dropped. This was going to be about Lu. "Just ask, Matthieu. I don't know if I can answer, but we won't know until you do." I moved into the open counterflow lane.

"Very well. I am confused about Lu's behavior. She is usually so decisive and yet now... well, she will not make up her mind about the wedding."

I was feeling cornered by my so-called friends. The fact that they all had relationships with people who were right here in Vancouver was bad enough when my guy was in Australia, but they all had problems. At least with Jake, when he was here, we floated along nicely. Yes, he occasionally wanted to talk about commitment and shit, but it never got to the point where we couldn't deal with it. Now, I was expected to be the love guru?

I pulled around a tourist bus and stayed with the traffic on the causeway. It wasn't heavy, but it seemed like everyone on the road was either a truck, bus, or new driver. It made for a slow pace.

"Charity, you can say no if you are uncomfortable." Matthieu's tone didn't match his words. He was really worried.

"I don't know how I can help. You and Lu always seemed fine." It felt like a cop-out. Lu was my best friend and we'd been through some tough times together, but Matthieu had changed me from an amateur to a professional — maybe was changing me is a more accurate statement. I owed them both and the best way to pay them back, in my opinion, was to keep out of their love life. Especially since I'd already tried to butt out with Lu. But I also knew that was more about me avoiding a discussion. "What exactly is happening?"

"I cannot get her to say what she wants for the wedding. I do not know what is expected."

Frustrating. I guess getting married is in the top ten of stressful life events for a reason. I intended to avoid it as long as possible and hoped that 'as long as possible' lasted until after my death. That said, maybe I could do a little sneaky information gathering for Lu. "What kind of wedding do you want, Matthieu?"

He sighed and I pictured his usual shrug accompanying the sound. "I just want to please Lu."

Given the way my call with her had gone, I guessed it wasn't as easy as usual to make her happy. I couldn't tell either of them to lighten up because there was clearly a problem underneath this that I didn't have time — or wine — enough to dig into. Maybe I'd just get them together when I had Mickey back with Iain. I knew why Lu was so freaked out. After her husband died, she went into a dry spell that lasted longer than her marriage. I never thought she'd even recognize a flirtation again. Then we'd gone to France, and Matthieu came on the scene. Pretty much from the first glance, I knew they were going to get together. If my guess was right, Lu was afraid he'd die when they got married. So, the wedding had to be perfect because it would have to survive the grief. Not rational, but then love isn't known for being rational.

"What was your first wedding like?"

"We went to city hall. It is common in France to have a civil service."

"And is that what you want?"

"I don't know, Charity. What do I do?"

Matthieu's first wife had died as well, but after a long illness not suddenly like Lu's husband. I wondered if he was harboring the same fears as Lu.

"You have to talk to her. And you need to stop trying to please her until you know what both of you want."

He chuckled. "I was hoping for some advice I couldn't make up myself."

"There is one thing you could do," I said. I pulled the car into a parking spot and turned it off. "You could get someone to play the mother-in-law. Then she'd take over the whole thing like the last time Lu did this. Then you can both sit back and complain about someone making all the decisions."

This time his laugh was loud and long. "That is a unique idea. It's unfortunate that we don't have parents."

"I'm sure Delores would be happy to fill in," I said. Delores

would do a great job, I'm sure. She'd fill the role of bossy organizer, and as I'd found out in my first case, she was capable of
being kind and caring.

"Perhaps I will find the courage to suggest this to Lu."

"Good luck." It was nice to feel like I was helpful for a
change.

FIFTEEN

The location of the ransom drop was a park surrounded by houses in various states of repair or disintegration. This was an area of the city I didn't spend much time in. It was not quite up-and-coming, and not quite falling apart. The houses were all old, some around a hundred years. It used to be a low-cost rental area, hippies and other people who didn't buy into the whole downtown lifestyle lived here. Families, at least enough of them to support an elementary school, stuck around, and there were small parks scattered throughout the area, causing confusion for people who assumed that they could drive from A to B without going around to C or even Y.

This block had two houses that were being restored. They stood out like well-landscaped, freshly painted sore thumbs.

I sat in my car waiting for the action. The note said to meet the dognappers at the swings in the park. There was no one there. I checked my watch; there was no way I'd missed them. Iain was supposed to arrive in five minutes. I guess they wanted to make sure he was alone before coming out of hiding.

While I waited, I checked my camera so I could save time at the warehouse. That surveillance was definitely feeling like a chore now. Despite myself, and Iain's lack of cooperation, I was fully engaged in finding Mickey. Plus, I wanted to make sure that he was okay after the chip removal.

The camera battery was fully charged. Checking it had become a compulsion since I missed the money shot one time because of a dead battery. I took a few pictures of the area to make sure I had the flash off and other settings ready for undercover work. All of this took ten minutes. No one showed up. No kidnappers. No Iain. Not even residents on an after-dinner walk.

There were two options. First that the people who took Mickey had sent a new location after Iain headed out. That might make sense because it would throw anyone following him off the trail. It was common in any number of detective shows on TV and maybe the dognappers had learned their trade from reruns. Or, Iain had deliberately sent me to the wrong place.

I would never put up with Iain's behavior if it wasn't for Mickey. I had a process for taking on clients and this one did nothing but remind me why I always stuck to it. I couldn't tell Iain to get lost, Mickey might suffer for it. I'm not a dog person, but I'm not heartless.

Normally, a client would do everything they needed to do to get the case closed. The usual problem I had was the client not knowing they had information I needed. That's why I interviewed people up front. With Iain, I'd missed the opportunity to interview him, and he seemed determined to make the case fail. If I hadn't seen him with Mickey, I would think he didn't care, but he loved that dog.

A couple of kids rode by me on bikes. They looked at me and into the back of my car as they went by. Maybe it was just curiosity, but I wasn't leaving my car, so if they were casing it, they'd be disappointed.

Now I had to make a decision. Leave Iain to his own problems and go work for my other clients or buckle down and stop letting Iain run the show.

I'm not a quitter.

There was something else going on, and I needed a partner to find out what that was. Matthieu was off the list. If I gave them the opportunity, I knew he and Lu would let me be the reason they didn't solve their wedding problems. That left Val.

SIXTEEN

She'd had time to cool off from our last encounter. Well, I'd had time to cool off. I hoped it was enough for her.

"Charity, what do you want?"

So much for her cooling off. I made a vow that I wasn't going to react to her snippiness. "What are you doing right now?"

"Trying to figure out what I can do about Rory." She sounded bored with the topic, that could work in my favor.

"How about something more interesting?"

"Are you saying my life isn't interesting?"

I rolled my eyes. "Your life is more interesting than it needs to be. I meant right now. Rather than mooning over whether or not you'll move in with a great guy who loves you, would you like to do some detective work?" As soon as I said it, I regretted the wording. Somehow, despite my determination to be calm, irritation had crept into the words. I heard it and there was no way Val would miss it.

"Yeah, he's a great guy. I'm not sure why he wants to move in with me." The drama was all gone. This time Val meant it.

Now I felt like an asshole. With Lu, it was easy to guess why she was having problems. With Val, she was always so self-assured that I forgot how her history could affect her relationships.

"Are you worried that he'll leave you?" I looked at my watch again. Crap, I didn't have time for this right now. But I didn't want to leave her feeling like this either.

"Yes, Dr. Freud, I fear that everyone in my life will abandon me because Emma left — twice." The words were laced with sarcasm, but the little hitch on the end told me it was fake, and she was fighting tears.

Her parents had been slaughtered; her sister had left her. Her life as a prostitute didn't create the kind of relationships that lasted more than an hour.

"I'm still here," I said, trying to sound like I wasn't in a rush.

"You want me to meet you for the surveillance?" Clearly the subject had changed.

"I can't wait for you to get there. I was thinking that you could try to find Iain for me." I told her about the note.

"How will I do that?" She seemed interested now.

"You could check on his house, and maybe see if he's at work."

"So, boring stuff."

"Surveillance is boring."

"Yeah, but we could talk if I was there."

She didn't want to help as much as she wanted to hang out. That made me feel guilty, like I'd abandoned her too. Val was going for all the emotional buttons this time. "We could meet for pizza afterward." It felt like a bribe. Like I was trying to get her to do her chores with a reward of ice cream.

"I've got another call, hang on."

While I waited for her to come back on the line, I stowed the camera, pulled on my seatbelt, and started the car.

"That was Rory. He's coming over. Sorry I guess I can't do your work for you."

I bit down on the words that would make it worse. Usually she was all too willing to get involved, but it was better for her to be with Rory than complaining about him to me.

"No problem. Have fun." I ended the call before she could say something smart-assed that would spoil my mood even more.

I was on my own, and I needed to deal with a real client now. One who didn't disappear or send me on a wild goose chase. I put the car in drive and sent a wish out to whoever was controlling my luck today that tonight I would get the picture I needed so I could close one case.

SEVENTEEN

Sometimes when I have to sit and observe people, I have a hard time finding a hiding place. On TV, and in the movies, there's always a doorway, or darkened fire escape, or convenient bushes. In real life, most people looking to make their business safe take the advice of security specialists and keep the entrances to their homes, and workplaces, clear and well lit. This warehouse was the exception. Yes, the loading bay was clear and well lit, but the fence around the lot was covered in ivy, and it was only a two-truck bay, so the space I had to cover with the camera was not that big. The ivy on the fence was thick enough to hide my car, and it allowed me to get comfortable while I waited. The sun wasn't completely down, but close enough. There were plenty of shadows to keep me, if not hidden, at least not easily seen.

I moved leaves aside to give me a peephole, and a way to take pictures when I needed to. Yes, I had to crouch and that would make it hard to get up, but this wasn't a chase type of situation. I just had to take a picture or three and leave.

The warehouse filled the block on one side, an apartment building sat at the far end on the other side. I was in enough shadow that someone in the apartments would have to know I was there in order to see me. Parking on the street was worth the risk, because it meant that my car wasn't alone and obvious. There were three other vehicles parked along the road. One had come in a few minutes after me. And in my previous nights, there had been no traffic along after seven, and it was after nine now. People in this neighborhood came home and stayed there, I guess.

The delivery truck was already there when I settled. Everything was on track for a normal night. I didn't know too much about the business of delivering stock to a warehouse, but I was sure that the goal was to be efficient. The fact that the truck sat there for almost half an hour before the bay doors opened made me suspicious. That driver got paid by the trip; he wouldn't be happy to wait.

I was starting to get the tingle in my gut that came with the knowledge I was about to get the money shot. The final steps to closing the case. It was my favorite part of being a PI. You sat around a lot, you filled out paperwork, but the magic second when you knew that you had the evidence you needed, that made all the boring stuff worthwhile.

My target opened the bay doors, hopped down, and walked along to the driver. He got out, walked to the back of the truck, and opened the rolling door. This was the point where I needed to see packages going anywhere but inside the warehouse.

Tonight, I was positioned a little better than before. I could see the back of the truck, and most of the area people would walk through. The only way to get a better view was to be inside the warehouse. That was my next step if this didn't work. Being inside was much more risky. I could get caught, or I could get locked in. And getting inside was easier during the day, which meant hours of waiting between everyone leaving and the truck showing up.

I watched as they started unloading. A small forklift was positioned at the edge of the bay. My target started pulling boxes from the back of the truck and loading them onto the forklift. I started taking pictures so I would have a timeline, maybe it would give my client some ideas of how to beef up security.

As soon as the forklift was full, the driver pulled away. Then my target reached into the back of the truck and pulled out a box. It was heavy by the way his knees took the weight. He said something to the driver, and then walked to his car to put the loot in the trunk. When he came back, he handed the driver an envelope. I didn't need him to open it to know that it was stuffed with cash.

I kept taking pictures until the truck pulled away and the bay door slammed shut. There could be a good reason for what I'd seen, but I doubted it. The box in the back of the car was exactly like the ones that went into the warehouse.

For the first time today, I felt like I knew what I was doing.

EIGHTEEN

Alone on the street, I made sure that the photos were on the chip, stowed the camera safely in the trunk and then called my client.

"I hate that we were right about him," he said in his gravelly voice.

My client was a nice guy and the thought that one of his employees was stealing hurt him. I admired his outlook even if I thought he should have learned better in the forty years he'd been in business.

"I'll send you the photos tomorrow. It's up to you how you handle it." I just supplied the evidence. It didn't matter to me what the client did with it — well, within legal limits. I would call the cops in a heartbeat if I thought any of my clients were going to take things into their own hands.

"I'm pretty sure I have to can him. Thanks, you do good work."

It was good to hear. I did my usual ask for a referral before we hung up. It was too late to do anything else. Maybe Iain had Mickey. I could check when I got back, but then it was a glass of wine, a pizza and something on TV until I fell asleep.

I started the car and pulled out onto the empty road. There was plenty of traffic on Prior, but it wouldn't slow me down much. At this time of night, I should be home in fifteen minutes.

As I reached the corner to turn into the stream of traffic, another vehicle started up and headed in my direction. I wouldn't normally have noticed, but two things prickled at my private eye spidey senses. First, no one had walked to the car, I would have noticed, and second, it was the same car that followed me in. A beige Ford sedan. If I let it get closer, I could get the license plate and model, but I wasn't in the mood for a confrontation, so I'd just drive away and check the information when I got home.

There was always a chance that it was all coincidence, but Matthieu was fond of saying that it's hard to tell the difference between coincidence and proof until someone gets hurt. And Jake was just as fond of saying that I got hurt too often. If my target, or someone he worked for, suspected that he was being watched, this could be a couple of goons who'd been hired to take the evidence and scare the PI.

Regardless, no way was I letting them follow me home. Pulling out onto Prior, I sped up a bit and changed lanes. If it was a coincidence, they would turn the other way, or they wouldn't speed up to catch me.

The car made the turn in my direction, and then changed lanes to get behind me.

I had a few options from this road. I could head over to Main Street and draw them past the cop shop. Or I could turn south and see how far they would follow me.

The latter would give me more time to be sure. And I knew that keeping them away from my home was probably futile. If they knew I'd be at the warehouse, they knew where I lived. The logic didn't help me deal with the feeling that I could keep my home a safe haven. I turned south on Main. The light at

Terminal was red, I took the opportunity of a space between two cabs and switched lanes. If I could get a glimpse of the driver, I'd have more information.

At the light, the car pulled up in the lane beside me, but didn't come forward enough for me to see who was inside. I just managed to see that there was only a driver, and that he was a man. Unless a passenger was lying down in the back seat, I could probably manage to deal with one man if it came to that. Still not enough proof that he was following me, but now I could take some maneuvers that would settle my mind. I would be happy to be wrong.

I switched to the right lane at 16th and got ready to get off Main in a quick turn. The car followed me into the turning lane.

I made the right on 18th and he followed.

I made a left on Quebec, the car stayed with me.

I saw a parking space a half block down the street. A rare thing on a Vancouver street at night. If I was going to park, I'd be looking for a 'residents only' sign, but I'd be pulling out as fast as I parked. I stopped beside the space as though I was going to parallel park. He had to wait for me, and that would give me a good look at his face.

I slid into the spot and held up a hand in thanks for his patience. He nodded in typical Vancouver fashion — like he was saying 'you didn't give me a choice, but you're welcome' and then sped to the end of the road and turned right. He'd looked like an average white guy.

It didn't settle me down. He could be driving around the block to wait for me to leave. He could have realized he'd been caught and decided to try again another day. He could just have been going in the same direction as me.

Crap.

I pulled out and hit the gas. At the next corner, I turned south and joined traffic on Main. If he was going around the block, he'd be too late. At King Edward, I took the right, and then headed home, keeping an eye out for the beige sedan.

When I parked my car, I made sure it was tucked between two SUVs and hidden from easy view of the entrance. If Mr. Beige came along, he'd have to go inside to find me. And maybe I could get something off the security cameras.

When I closed the gate to our community, I ran down and knocked on Iain's door, but no one answered. The other houses were dark and closed up, making me feel like I was the only person awake on the dock.

I tried to tell myself that it was all part of the job, that I had a good security system, that I could handle myself. It didn't work. Now that I was alone, the bravado melted under the fear.

NINETEEN

The next morning, I woke up to the sound of yelling from one of the live-aboard boats on the next dock. The couple were waiting for repairs to their engine before continuing on a round-the-world trip. I didn't hold out much hope for their success on getting the whole way, since they'd spent most of the time at the dock screaming at each other. What would they do when they were in the middle of the ocean with nowhere to go?

I didn't want to waste a lot of time, so I showered, and then ate my toast as I got dressed. It was still early enough that Iain should be home, and I was going to talk to him whether he wanted to deal with me or not.

Twenty minutes after waking up I was knocking on Iain's door. No answer, and no barking. Mickey definitely wasn't home, but I wasn't sure about Iain. Would he be at work by now? It was only seven a.m., and he'd been working late last night. I banged on the door again, then put my ear to it.

I heard voices, then music; a radio. I didn't care much what the neighbors would think of the racket, I needed to get inside and talk to Iain.

I hammered the door and started yelling. "Iain, I know you are in there, open up."

I leaned against the door again, no radio now. Someone was home, and Iain lived alone. I raised my fist to start all over, then I heard the lock click and the handle turned.

"Iain isn't home," a woman's voice said through the crack.

"Do you know where he is? I'm trying to find Mickey for him." I made my voice kind and warm, hoping she'd ignore the previous yelling. "It's really important."

The door stayed closed, but she asked, "Who are you?"

"I'm Charity. I live down there," I said, pointing to my house even though I wasn't sure she could see the action. "I'm a PI. Iain hired me to find Mickey."

I must have made a positive impression because she opened the door wide. "Iain went to pay the ransom last night, and he hasn't come home."

What I should have said, was 'do you know where he went', but I was shocked into asking "Sara Lyman?"

My client's missing wife was standing inside Iain's home. Her picture didn't do her any favors. She was model beautiful. I'm sure she looked even better when she wasn't in sweats and a hoodie, but even slobbed out, her skin was fine and smooth. Her eyes were that emerald green most people could only get from tinted contacts, and her hair was a cascade of blond curls that I would have killed for.

Her eyes narrowed and she looked me over from head to toe. "Do I know you?"

"No," I said cautiously. Was it better to just let her husband know where she was, or should I ask why she left? Or should I just concentrate on Mickey and get the hell away?

"But you know my name. How is that? We've been so careful."

I couldn't just let it go. "Can I come in?"

She looked down the finger dock. I knew there was no one on the street, but she didn't know the neighborhood.

"You don't want the neighbors hearing. Believe me there's at least one person watching us from behind the drapes."

She glanced at the houses again and then shrugged. "Sure, come on in."

TWENTY

I'd only been inside Iain's house once before. We were a small community, seven houses in total. We don't exactly socialize, but we do look out for each other. Iain's house looked like someone had just moved in, or a very localized tornado had hit it. Clothing and boxes were scattered around the living room. The small kitchen counter was littered with the contents of the cupboards. There wasn't a surface in sight without something balanced on top. The furniture wasn't where I expected it to be either. Was a couch useful facing the front door?

"Wow, is this Mickey's doing?"

Sara looked around. "No. So how do you know me?"

So, she wasn't going to be distracted. I had to keep my two objectives in mind, so she didn't get mad and kick me out. "Actually, before I get into that, do you know where Iain went? I think I should follow up with him if he's been out all night."

"He said he was leaving you a note," she said. Her entire body had tensed up since the door closed. She wasn't planning on giving up anything without a compelling reason.

"He did. No one showed up. I thought maybe he'd put the wrong address on the note. I have to tell you, the people who

took Mickey aren't just playing around. They cut out his chip."
Maybe the threat of violence against the dog would push her to
answer my question.

"Where did you go?"

I gave her the location and she sighed. "That's not what he
told me." She grabbed a napkin from the kitchen counter and a
pen from a drawer. "Here's where he said they told him to go."
She wrote an address and handed me the paper. "Now, how do
you know me?"

"When you left your husband, did you think he'd just move
on?" I watched her reaction. Not even the most experienced liar
could cover their tell if you looked close enough.

"We were having a lot of troubles. I didn't think he cared."

Not exactly helpful, but I did notice her glance at her ring
finger. There was no ring on it.

"He does care. Is there any reason I shouldn't go phone him
right now and tell him where you are?" I could hold out a little
longer, but I wasn't going to let her disappear again.

"No. I mean he didn't hurt me or anything." A glance at the
absent ring accompanied a slow blink, like she was holding back
tears. "Will you let me call him?" She asked it like she could talk
him into forgiving her if I didn't get there first.

"Why are you here, at Iain's?" I knew the answer. Iain had
lied about knowing her, and I wanted to see if she would lie too.

"I... we were having an affair. We needed to be very
discreet. I would have been reassigned if my company knew. I
liked the clients I had."

No glance at the ring this time. She didn't look at me,
though. It could have been shame, or a cover up. I didn't want
to take the time to find out. I looked at the note in my hand.
There was no way Iain would have made a mistake when he
left me the information. This was a completely different
location.

"Why didn't Iain call me last night instead of leaving a note?"

"I have no idea. He's nuts about that dog. I guess he was in a rush to get him back."

I had a feeling she knew exactly why, but it would take too long to get her to talk. "What's your cell number?"

She told me, and I dialed it to check. Her phone rang. So, this time she wasn't lying.

"I'll call you when I find something. You have until tonight to call your husband."

She nodded.

"If you run, I'll find you, Sara." I tried to keep my voice even, no threat intended, just a promise.

"Don't worry. I didn't run away from my husband. I ran to Iain. I'll be here when you get back."

Not completely convinced, I left her and headed out to retrieve my car.

TWENTY-ONE

When I got to my car, my phone rang: Val. "Hey," I said. New day, new attitude hopefully.

"Yeah, I guess I can help you out today if you need it."

That was a surprise. I could use her help, but I didn't want her running out on me at the last minute. "Don't you have any clients?"

"I got a couple of days before I start with my next project. I'm totally free, Charity. Do you want my help or not?" The noise in the background made it hard to identify her attitude. I know Val was offering help, but something made me wonder if there was more to it.

"Yeah, I have to go check on something. It might get ugly, are you ready for that?" I still didn't trust her change of heart.

"Come get me. I'm over on Granville and 49th."

That meant she was leaving Rory's place. His parents lived in the ritzy area of Vancouver. I guess being a highly sought-after lawyer paid the bills. Rance, Rory's dad, had done me a great favor last year with the cops. I liked him, but I understood why Rory rebelled against the establishment. There was no place in the field of criminal law for a kid who wanted to make movies.

"Hang on." I started the car and plugged in my earbuds. Maybe I should invest in a Bluetooth connection. "I'll be there in twenty minutes," I said. "Are you okay?"

"Yeah, yeah. I had a fight with Rory." A truck rumbled by on her end. "Call me when you get closer."

I didn't have a choice because she just ended the call.

I waited until I made the turn onto Granville at Davie before following orders.

I was going to have to hear about the fight anyway so instead of saying hi, I asked, "Was it bad?"

"I don't know. We never had a fight before."

I could tell she thought it was a bad fight, there was a little hitch in her voice when she talked. I didn't want her standing on Granville Street crying. "Everyone fights. You'll probably be okay. Tell me what it was about."

We had plenty of time to hash it through. I had to get through the rest of the downtown traffic and then I had half of the city to cross before I got to her. And then, we'd be driving from one side to another in distance, and economic status, before we got to the location Sara had given me.

"Rance, you know, Rory's dad? He offered me a contract with the law firm. They have to move a bunch of old records into digital. He figured my skills would be good for it. And it was great money."

"Rory didn't want you to do it?" Maybe this fight was less about Rory and Val and all about Rory and his dad.

"He said that his dad was just trying to buy me."

I liked Rory, I really did, but he could be totally clueless. You don't tell a girl who used to work the streets that a man is trying to buy her. Rory knew her past, but he didn't understand it.

"What did you say?"

"I didn't hit him or anything, don't worry. I said I was running a business and Rance would be a good client, and that he was just trying to help out." Another truck went by. "He didn't know what he'd said, Charity, and I don't want you telling him. My past is past."

She tried very hard to make that true. "So, where does the fight come in?" I was out of the Granville Street shopping area and had a clear run to her now. "I'm almost there."

"Good. He said if I was going to take Rance's money for a job, then I should be happy to stay in his house. He is so unreasonable." This time I heard the pain and annoyance clearly.

I could understand both sides of the problem. Val was trying to hang on to her independence at the same time as she took a big step in trusting Rory. Rory didn't see the sense in sharing the kind of place they could afford if Rance was happy to have them live at home. It was something they would have to work out. I was certain that Val's version was skewed. But Rory probably didn't understand the underlying message about taking money for work. It was normal in his world, mine too. In Val's it might have a different feeling.

I saw her on the corner, looking tiny and alone. "Running away isn't the best way to solve it," I said as I slowed the car.

She waved and ended the call.

I pulled off Granville to stop, and Val joined me in the car. "I'm not running away; I'm helping you out."

I laughed. Val could always find a way to get the last word in even in the middle of a conversation. I drove down the quiet tree lined streets of Shaughnessy. This was the old money side of town and the houses were big, stone, and mostly hidden behind old growth hedges that had been carefully shaped over years into a green wall.

I took advantage of the slower drive as we made our way

toward 16th where I could get us headed east again without hazarding a left turn across the commuter traffic, and then continued the topic. "If that's true, you'll need to start talking to him again soon."

She huffed and then picked up her phone to check for messages. "I know. I'm just not ready to figure out a real answer to his question."

"That's mature." I tried not to sound too surprised. "What makes you think there's a real answer?"

"He's got a point. I don't think it's true. I think Rance's job is legit, but if he's doing it for any other reason, I won't take his money." She dropped her phone back into her bag and stared out of the window.

I turned onto 16th and the traffic increased. Did I want to get into it with Val? Not really. I didn't think Rance was going to offer Val work if it wasn't legit. He might offer it to her because she was Rory's girlfriend, but it would be a real job. I'd been surprised, given his reputation, at how he'd accepted Val into the family. Her past wasn't exactly stellar, but I guess Rance and his wife, were more about professional reputations than social ones. I never knew how to separate the two sides of my life.

"I will give you one piece of advice," I said. "Do you want it?"

Val turned to look at me. Her lips were tightly closed, but her eyes were suspiciously wet. The fight with Rory was taking more out of her than I realized.

"Well, I did ask," she said. "Not that you are the relationship guru, but what you have with Jake seems to work for you. Even if it looks weird to the rest of the world. And maybe it only works because you are never together."

I pulled into a parking space on the corner of a run-down street. The location I got from Sara was in the middle of a row of single-story houses that had probably been built in the fifties, and were barely maintained, let alone restored. "When you talk to Rory, listen for his side of it. I'm not sure he's the kind of kid who likes to live with his parents. There must be something else there."

She grunted agreement and got out of the car.

I didn't expect a thanks, but I couldn't seem to get anything right with Val recently. Maybe I'm just really bad at this advice business.

TWENTY-TWO

We walked up the concrete steps to the front door. The steps
had once been painted red, perhaps to cheer up the curb appeal
of the gray stuccoed house. Now there was more concrete
showing through than paint on the steps.

The front door had cobwebs draped across it. Whoever
lived here didn't come in this way and didn't care what the
spiders did to the look of the house. I made Val stand behind me
because I had a suspicion this place was either a grow op or a
meth lab. Not that my body would protect her from an explo-
sion, or a shotgun blast, but hey, it felt right.

"I'm guessing no one will answer," Val muttered.

I looked at the cobwebs and a shiver ran down my back.
"Hang on," I said, ignoring her pessimism. I dug a pen out of my
bag and used it to stir the webs like cotton candy. It still made
me feel like the spiders were crawling all over me, but at least I
didn't have to have sticky hands.

The webs clear, I rapped on the door with as much
authority I could manage. Then we waited. I was happy there
was no snarling bark from a guard dog, but the absence of doggy

greetings also meant there was no Mickey. Or at least no live Mickey.

"How long are we going to wait?" Val asked, already antsy.

If I was smart, it wouldn't take any time. I know Val meant how long before we went and did something more interesting. I couldn't just leave it here. Mickey was missing, and as far as I knew Iain was missing too. If not, why hadn't he gone home?

I sighed. "Let's take a look around the back. Maybe there's a window we can peek through, or maybe they are in the yard and can't hear us knocking."

Val rolled her eyes. I kept my face impassive. She didn't need to know that I agreed it was a lame plan. It was all I had.

The house was sitting in the middle of the lot, but the left side was barred with a chain link fence. The right side had the typical narrow concrete path, buckled, and covered with moss, but still passable. There was nothing to see through the small ground-level windows as we passed because each one was boarded up. There was a chain link gate at the end of the house, but it was hanging open on one hinge. My stomach was tingling. I like to think of it as my investigative gut, but it usually showed up when I was going to do something stupid, so it just might be fear instead.

"Stay here for a minute," I whispered to Val.

"You can't go in there alone," she hissed back.

It was really a no-win situation, but if I didn't have to worry about Val, I could be totally focused on the house and anything I found inside. If there was nothing, we'd wasted a few minutes. If there was something dangerous, one of us was still free to call the cops.

"If we both go, and something happens, there's no one to call for help." I hoped she wouldn't argue because I really needed to get this over with before I freaked out.

"Like when the ice-witch caught us both?" she asked, sarcasm dripping from every syllable.

Val was supposed to be on watch that time, but she'd left the safety of my car and been caught by Penelope Whitehall's thug. "No. Not like then, because you aren't going to get caught and dragged into the situation. You are going to stay alert and run away if anyone comes. You will call the police at any hint something has gone wrong."

Maybe the memory of how badly she'd been hurt the last time made her nod, but I believed her. She'd do as I asked, and if something went wrong, she'd remind me how stupid I was to leave her out of it. "I'm going to see if I can find anything that will lead me to Mickey or Iain. If it's safe, I'll call you."

"Fine, just don't disappear like they did."

I handed her my bag, taking my phone and Taser — a girl can't be too trusting when entering a strange house. "I promise I won't. Thanks for worrying."

She grinned. "Need a ride home." Then she spoiled the humor by hugging me.

"I won't leave you, Val." I knew that no matter how much she pretended otherwise, Val expected everyone to abandon her like Emma had done twice.

"Shut up and get going," she said, giving me a little shove toward the door.

TWENTY-THREE

The gate was open just enough for me to twist myself through without having to move it. If I had to leave in a hurry, I wouldn't worry about the noise. But I wasn't going to give anyone a heads up with the grating of metal against concrete as I came in.

The backyard was a mess of bare patches in weeds, like a pack of dogs had been digging and peeing all over. There was a concrete pad under the back stairs, but no other hard surface. The stairs themselves looked iffy. I tested the first one; despite appearances, it held my weight and didn't creak or groan. I could see that the back door had a window in it, and there was no curtain, or board, over it. The kitchen window on my side of the door, was a different story, boarded tight. That would work in my favor. No one inside would see me until I got to the top.

Halfway up one of the steps moved under my foot, and the nail holding it squealed. I stopped breathing. Sounds went quiet and I started to feel cold radiate from the center of my body. Then dizziness took over. My lungs forced me to gasp in a breath, making as much noise in my head as the stair.

I waited, but nothing happened. I waited a few more

seconds as my breathing got under control and my heart slowed. Val was not the only one who carried a little trauma from the Penelope Whitehall case.

I got to the back door without being attacked. Or yelled at by helpful neighbors. If anyone was watching, I would definitely look suspicious, but it seemed no one was, or perhaps no one cared.

The window was grimy, but I could make out what was inside. It was the kitchen as I expected; these houses had a predictable floor plan. The table was turned over, the only chair I could see was broken, the wood at the split still clean, so it happened recently. I caught a glimpse of the living room through the doorway. The couch was torn, and stuffing burst out like it was guts. No one could live here in this mess. I suspected that someone had been living here recently, though.

I ran down the stairs, no longer worried about the noise. Val was in the street waiting as agreed. It gave me hope that she'd learned to listen. I told her what I'd seen.

"So, what next?" she asked. "Do we break in to get some more clues?"

"I'm not sure. I think we should probably call the cops, but that won't help us find Mickey, or Iain. We could break in, but if there's something inside that the cops want to investigate, we'll contaminate the scene." That meant we'd be delayed until the police were satisfied that we hadn't committed any serious crimes.

Val stared at me as if willing me to make a decision. "I don't have all day, Charity."

I couldn't think straight, and Val's impatience wasn't helping. Something about this situation was ringing all my alarm bells, but I couldn't just walk away. Or, I couldn't just walk away without getting some advice of my own.

"Let me call Matthieu," I said. "He might have another idea." I was done with rushing around after false leads and feeling afraid. I realized that I didn't really need Matthieu's advice, just his different point of view.

TWENTY-FOUR

His line rang enough times that I thought I'd get his voicemail, but then I heard "Hey, Charity."

"Lu?"

"Yes. Matthieu isn't here right now."

I dreamed of a world where people would be there to answer my calls. When that happened, I'd start dreaming they would help.

"I need to talk to him about a case," I said. I knew that Lu might be able to throw a few ideas around. She'd been with me on a couple of cases, so she wasn't totally clueless about investigating. I just didn't want to bring her into it right now.

"He'll be back in an hour. I don't know how to reach him, since he left his phone here."

Something in Lu's voice made me wonder if they'd had a fight. Images of the calm Matthieu storming out of the house forgetting his phone ran through my mind.

I dismissed them. Lu and Matthieu didn't fight.

"Fine, I'll figure it out," I said, trying to let her off the hook. Then, because I'm a sucker, I added, "How did the talk go?"

She didn't answer right away, and that feeling they were in trouble came back. Weddings could be stressful, but most people made it through, even if it was just to get divorced later. "Lu?"

"I didn't get into it. I just told him I wanted a big wedding because I know that's what he wants. We're going to hire a wedding planner, and everything will be fine." The words came out in a rush, like she was trying to convince herself.

"Well, it's a solution." What else could I say? With Val standing there actually tapping her foot and checking her watch, I couldn't get into a long conversation about love. I also had a sinking feeling that if I didn't find Mickey soon, he wouldn't be found. "I have to go, Lu."

She changed the subject. "What did you want Matthieu for?"

"Advice on my case." I shook my head at Val who was reaching for the phone. "Tell him I found the real location, I think, and it looks like someone has ransacked the place. I'm going to go in." I gave her the address.

"That part of town? Don't do it. Call the cops." Lu didn't like me taking risks.

I get it, she's my friend. I want her to be safe too, but it's my job. As a PI, I had to take risks. But, then again, maybe I was naturally stubborn and contrary. "I have to find out what happened." If I didn't and it turned out Mickey was inside and hurting, I'd regret it every time I saw Iain.

Val had started walking to the car.

"People will be around, ask the neighbors. You'll be safer that way."

That was a great idea. I'd missed the fact that people living here didn't generally have nine-to-five jobs. "Brilliant. I'll go knocking on doors."

"Alone?"

"No, I have Val. If something goes wrong, one of us will call for help." I would make sure we weren't both in the line of fire if it came to that.

"Fine. I'll let Matthieu know."

The call ended.

TWENTY-FIVE

"We'll see if anyone knows the occupants," I said, trying to sound professional. It was more for my sake than Val's. Getting my brain to switch from friend to private investigator and back was getting harder every time. I was well aware that I wasn't doing a bang-up job with the friend part, but I could fix that — with a lot of wine and effort. Not getting the caseload cleared would hurt my business.

Val looked up and down the street. "I don't know if anyone will talk to us." Then, looking at me with a grin, she added, "Maybe we can bust some noses to make our point."

I laughed at her tough guy act. She was all of five-two, and even soaking wet in a fur coat she wouldn't be hard to pick up. "Let's try being nice first."

"You are no fun anymore." She crossed the lawn, well, more just a weedy patch of dirt, and marched up the steps to the neighbor's door.

I followed, suddenly worried that she'd take out her frustrations on whoever answered the door. "Let me do all the talking." I knocked.

"Then why am I here?"

"Company."

After a couple of rounds of knocking, no one came, and no sounds inside. I couldn't go nosing around in the backyard of every house on the block, so we just moved on.

The next two houses were as fruitless as the first. This was the frustrating part of the job. I had more sympathy for Val as she grudgingly followed me up the steps of the third house.

This time my knock was answered with a deep barking and someone yelling at the dog to shut up. The door opened and we were presented with a skinny guy in a stained wife-beater and yellow basketball shorts. I didn't have to see his teeth to know he was an addict. He scratched at his arms like there were cockroaches crawling under there. Behind him, standing stiff legged and producing a low growl was a pit bull. Welcome to the stereotype.

I heard Val slide behind me on the step below, as if I could protect her if the dog decided to attack.

"Hi, my name is Charity Deacon —."

"You a cop?" his voice was cracked.

"I'm a private investigator. I'm trying to find the people who live down the street at number 3427." I paused this time. I don't like to be interrupted, but I needed him to be talking.

"Yeah, I don't care what the neighbors do." He scratched his belly for a change. "It's not like they can bring down the tone of the neighborhood." He gave a little dry laugh at his own joke.

"So, you wouldn't know anything about a break-in?" Even in his state, it was hard to believe he wouldn't have heard the noise that must have been going on.

"Nope, keep my nose in my own business."

The dog gave another bark. My lack-of-informant turned around and yelled at it again. If it hadn't been thirsting for my blood, I would have felt some pity for it.

"Here's my card. If you think of anything call me."

He took my card and turned it over as though there was a secret on the back. Then he reached for the door. "I won't."

I thanked him and turned to go.

"Hey. Try across the street. The place with the green door. That guy watches everything. It's like being under the warden's gaze when I go out." He shut the door before I could say anything.

"That was nice," Val snarked. "We should call the SPCA. That dog shouldn't have to put up with the abuse."

"Yelling at the dog isn't abuse. It's just nasty."

"That dog didn't get mean because he was treated nicely. Charity, we need to call someone." She kept looking over her shoulder.

"I didn't know you cared that much about dogs." That sounded callous even to me.

"What? I have to be a dog lover to think it's wrong to make a dog act mean like that?"

She was right but calling the SPCA would get the dog put down more than likely; viscous dogs didn't get a chance to explain. "Maybe he needs protection. Maybe the dog is all bark. We need to concentrate on Mickey. Let's see if Mr. Green Door is in. If he gives us a reason to call the SPCA, we'll do it right away."

She followed me across the street without arguing.

The door was answered on the first knock, like the man was standing waiting for us.

I introduced myself and Val, who was standing beside me this time. He returned the courtesy. Mr. Ozwald was in his late sixties by my guess. He was neatly dressed in gray slacks and a white shirt with a burgundy sweater on top. His expression was perfectly suspicious; eyes narrowed, mouth pressed shut. This wasn't likely to end up in a major clue for the case.

TWENTY-SIX

I figured getting right to the point would stop him from just shutting the door on us. "I'm on a case and I need to talk to the guys who live there." I pointed to the ransacked house.

"You'd better come in then." He didn't wait for an answer, just shuffled to the back of the house.

"Think he's lived here forever?" Val whispered.

"Long enough that I remember when this was a good working-class neighborhood, young lady," he said over his shoulder.

Val blushed. "Sorry."

He pointed to two vinyl and metal chairs at the kitchen table. The whole room looked like it was set up as a nineteen sixties movie set. Everything was clean and tidy and well maintained.

"What do you want to know about those two vandals?"

I pulled out a notebook, partly to take notes, and partly because I figured he expected it. "I'll be honest. I need to talk to them about a dog they took. My client got a ransom note, and as far as I can see, he came to that house to pay. Now he's missing and the dog is still gone."

"Tea?" Mr. Ozwald asked.

"I'll make it," Val said jumping up from her seat. "You can give Charity all the information you have."

He seemed surprised at her offer but told her where to find the teabags and cups. I knew a few people like him, made judgments right away and they were always bad. In this neighborhood, I figure he was also almost always right. It was nice to see he was willing to accept something beyond first impressions.

"Have you seen a strange dog with them?" I asked. "A black lab?"

He nodded. "They are Terry and Mick, don't know the last names. Yep, they've had a few dogs with them lately. The black lab was the most recent."

I made the note. The kettle whistled and Val poured boiling water into three mugs.

"Milk or sugar?" she asked. It was interesting to see this side of her. She was putting him at ease so I could get what I needed. This was the business side of Val. Maybe she only showed the bratty side to me.

"Always take it black, young lady. Now, what else do you need to know?"

His suspicion had melted under Val's care. I was definitely going to ask her to be more like that with me. I guess Mr. Ozwald was just lonely and stuck in a neighborhood of people he considered criminals.

"I peeked in the back window," I admitted. "I know that's not polite, but I was worried. The place looks like it's been tossed. Did you hear or see anything about that?" It was a fine balance between interrogation and gossip. I hoped Mr. Ozwald didn't take umbrage because I focused on the questions rather than the niceties.

He stared into his tea, making a decision.

"I don't think anyone is going to come after you," I added.

He looked up at me. "It's not that, young lady. I've been

taking care of myself longer than you've been alive. I know they all think I'm nosy, but I figure the more I know about the people who live here the safer I am. I've never called the cops, and I'm not likely to start doing it as long as they keep their business out of my property."

I nodded and waited for him to decide what to tell me.

After a few minutes, he started talking. "The two you are asking about get in a lot of scrapes. They always have a dog and they don't seem to know how to be the alpha so to speak."

I nodded again and made a few notes.

"Last night they had two visitors. The first one was a nice-looking fella. I remember wondering what he was doing around here. One of them, Terry I think, met him at the car and took him around the back. A few minutes later another car pulled up. Tall guy, maybe late thirties, brown hair. He just walked around the back and let himself in."

The first visitor must have been Iain.

"This second guy, did you get his license plate?"

"I didn't. He had one of them Hummers. License plate was covered in mud. I remember thinking that he was in for a ticket if the police noticed."

"How was he dressed?" I asked.

Mr. Ozwald's expression closed up.

"She doesn't mean to just interrogate you, Mr. O," Val said. "It's just Mickey, the dog, has been missing a long time and we need to find him."

Her words softened him, and he continued. "He was wearing a black sweater, them yellow kind of khaki pants, no jacket, nothing special; all kind of looked new, though."

"Thanks. You never know what will make the difference," I said.

"There was something. I remember thinking he was a cocky bastard, if you'll excuse the expression. Something about the way he strode into the backyard. As if he owned the world. You know what I mean?"

"Yeah. I've met a few of those people," I said, grinning. "It's nice when I can bring them down."

He laughed, a short bark of sound that lifted ten years from his face. "I reckon it is. Anyway, there was some yelling, and I'm pretty sure I heard a dog. Then the second guy comes out and drives away. That's all I saw."

I looked at Val. We both knew that meant something bad had happened. "There was no one there when we looked."

He drank the last of his tea. "The first car was gone when I got up this morning. I sleep pretty heavy, so they all could have left in the middle of the night." He looked at both of us in turn. "You should call the police. I don't want to be responsible for you getting hurt."

I closed my notebook and waited while Val cleared the tea dishes. It was too soon to call the police. I needed a look inside that house.

"We won't get hurt, Mr. Ozwald. It won't be the first time we've gone into what might be a dangerous situation."

My words didn't seem to impress him. They didn't set my nerves to rest either. But he didn't argue. I had the feeling he was going to be watching and would break his pattern of not calling the cops if we didn't come out of the house fast.

TWENTY-SEVEN

"I don't really want to go in there," Val said as we trooped across the street.

"You can wait in the car," I offered.

"No." She grabbed my arm to stop me advancing. "I meant, both of us. I don't want you going in there either. I have a bad feeling about this. And I don't want to die knowing the last thing I did with Rory was fight."

Dramatic.

Well, she did have a point. Our record with dangerous situations didn't inspire confidence. "It's not like with Penelope."

She stood her ground and glared at me. "How do you know? It's an old house that needs a lot of work. There's been some kind of shit going on. Mickey isn't... there."

I knew what she'd left out in that pause — *Mickey isn't alive if he's there.* I wasn't going to argue, first because she was right and it was dangerous, and also because I didn't have a choice. If Iain was there, tied up or worse, I had to help him. I had to know what was there.

"Val, we just need to look. It will be different this time,

because we'll both be on alert. If we find anything, we're out of there and dialing 911."

She pulled out her phone. "I'm texting Rory. You should text Jake. At least if something goes wrong, we won't leave them wondering."

That was a sweet idea and it wouldn't take more than a second. Jake would probably be shooting a scene or something, so unlikely to get back to me. I pulled out my phone and sent him a series of heart emoticons.

To my surprise, he answered right back. *Me too. We should talk later.* Jake had never quite gotten the hang of emoticons. He needed a teenager in his life.

I tucked my phone back into my bag. Val tapped hers once and smiled.

"Okay, let's go," she said with more enthusiasm than before.

"Hang on." I headed for the car. "We should be prepared."

Val stood beside me at the trunk, peering over my shoulder. "You have a gun or something?"

I reached in and took out a small black carryall. "No, but I have a big flashlight that might come in handy. And I need my lock picks."

I handed her the second flashlight.

"Rory says hi."

"Nice. How much did you tell him?" It might be helpful for him to know where we went missing — not that I was planning for that to happen.

She glared like I'd asked if she had permission to come. "He's not in charge of me."

"I know, but I'm curious. You wanted me to give you advice. It might be easier if I know more about him." Not that I was planning to give in and actually give her advice.

She tossed her purse into the trunk. "I told him what we know and what we're going to do."

"What did he say?" I was interested in how they would handle it when Val did something like this. It's not like she was officially my assistant, but I got the feeling she liked investigations enough that eventually she'd want to work with us full time.

Jake and I had argued a few times about the danger, usually when I was in the hospital after getting beaten up. Eventually he'd given up arguing. After that, his expression did all the talking.

Val hefted the flashlight. "Babe, I hate it when you do this stuff, but it's kind of hot. Be safe."

"He's a keeper." I tucked my keys, phone, and picks into my jacket pocket. I reached for the box of latex gloves, but it was empty, I needed to get better at keeping that stuff in stock. I couldn't do much about it now, so I slammed the trunk.

"Yeah, maybe." She looked over her shoulder at the house. "Let's get this over with. I need to get back to my life."

I guess I was off the hook for love advice.

Val followed me down the side of the house. This time I didn't care if I made noise going up the stairs. I was more interested in speed than stealth.

The lock on the door was new and high quality, something I hadn't noticed before. Why add a lock like that to a door that would splinter under a good kick? I kept the question to myself, because I knew Val would use it as a reason to stop what we were doing. I knew that because I was already wondering if we should walk away.

I sniffed, but I didn't smell skunk or ammonia, so no grow op or meth lab. I picked the lock and gave the door a shove. It swung open about a foot and a half. Enough room for us to squeeze through.

"Watch out for the chair," I told Val as I stepped over the broken leg that stuck up from the second kitchen chair.

Whoever made this mess had shifted the other one until it was jammed between the upturned table and the door to the basement.

"We should have gloves," Val said. "We don't want our fingerprints all over this place."

"I'm out of them. If there's a reason to take fingerprints, we'll tell the cops what happened. If we don't find anything suspicious, it doesn't matter."

She huffed and pulled out a white cloth. As she shook it out, I saw RM embroidered on the corner. "I'll wipe them off as we go. No need to take chances." She turned to wipe the lock.

"Wait. If you clean up now, you might destroy some important evidence."

"Fine. If we don't find anything, I'll clean on our way out. I'm not touching anything. I don't want my prints here for the cops to find in the future."

It was a good plan. "Why do you have one of Rance's handkerchiefs?"

She looked at the cloth and laughed. "You have to promise not to tell."

I took a deep breath and told myself it wasn't my business. "Promise."

She was having trouble telling me through the giggles. "It's not Rance's. It's Rory's."

I started laughing with her. Rory was currently sporting what he thought was an indie look, baggy pants, graphic tee-shirts and a leather jacket. Not the kind of look that went with linen handkerchiefs.

"Okay, I won't tell. We need to go downstairs. So, you keep an eye on what I touch, and then you'll know what to clean." I waited for her to nod before pushing the table aside and lifting the broken chair onto the top so the back and basement doors were clear. I closed the back door and opened the basement.

The smell of urine and feces wasn't strong, but it was there. I guess they kept the dogs in the basement.

The light switch was just inside the door. I flipped it on and looked inside. Narrow stairs led to a concrete floor. It was very much like the place where Penelope had tried to kill us. All the pain and fear of that came rushing at me. I put my hand on the wall to steady me while I got my control back.

If I was feeling the echoes of that event, Val was too. "You don't have to come down, Val."

Her breathing shuddered. "No. I'll come."

I led the way. The smell got stronger, but I couldn't see any evidence of a dog. Halfway down, I got a view of the whole basement. "Val, go back up. Now!"

"Why?"

"I said go!"

I waited until she stomped back to the kitchen before continuing down.

TWENTY-EIGHT

There were three bodies in the far corner of the basement.

I didn't want to, but I had to know for sure. I put my hands in my pockets, so I wouldn't accidentally leave trace evidence, and held my breath. Stepping as close as I could, I crouched down beside the largest of the three. Yep. It was Iain. I had to assume the other two were the dognappers.

There was no sign of Mickey.

My lungs wanted air, so I ran to the stairs where the smell was less intense.

"Are you okay?" Val called down.

I rushed up the stairs and pulled her outside.

"Wait, I need to wipe your prints."

I gulped in clean air and dug in my pocket for my phone. "No, we need to call the police." I handed her my keys and the lock picks. There was no need to be caught with B&E tools. "Put these and the flashlights in the trunk and bring our purses. We found the door open, okay?"

"Yeah. We were looking for the dog, and we got worried about the mess and the fact that the door was open, so we looked inside."

Val was an expert at building a story with just enough truth to make it real. The door being open was the key to our innocence here. "Keep to that, no need for complications." I gave her a little push toward the car, pressing *emergency call* on my phone.

I gave the 911 operator all the details and told her I would stick around to answer questions.

I knew better than to leave. They could trace the call back to my phone faster than I could get home. For a regular person, that wouldn't be a problem. A regular person could claim they were frightened about what would happen to them, so they took off. A PI couldn't do that. At best the cops would become more uncooperative; at worse they would make every case I took too hard to deal with.

I joined Val at the car. "You want to go?" There was a bus stop a few blocks south of us.

"I'll stick around. You might need someone to back you up." She gave me back my keys. "You have anything to drink? That tea just made me more thirsty."

My water supply was coming in handy again.

Val looked at the plastic bottle, turning it on its side. "No soda?"

"Sorry. Soda doesn't store well in a trunk." I half expected a lecture on using plastic bottles. "We shouldn't be long. How about lunch?"

"You think they'll feed us at the station?"

That wasn't my actual plan. "I meant at a restaurant. If they want us to go to the station, they can wait until we're ready."

She took a long drink. Then we both turned toward the sound of sirens in the distance. I guess 911 considers three dead bodies an emergency. I figured there was no reason for the noise since the killer wasn't around, and the bodies weren't getting any deader.

"Should I call Rory's dad?" Val sounded worried.

I couldn't afford Rance's rates, nor did I want to rack up a favor debt with him. "Let's see how it goes. If they start asking about more than just what we saw, we'll ask for a lawyer."

The sirens were still faint, so we still had a couple of minutes before the official processes took over. Time to get our story, maybe not straight, but at least aligned.

"Let's leave Mr. Ozwald out of it," I said.

Val frowned at me like I was the killer and wanted her to lie for me. "Why? He just told us some information." She glanced at his door and I followed, a curtain shifted back into place. "You don't think maybe he did it?"

"No, but I want to make sure he's not targeted. The neighbors won't like that he brought the cops to the street."

"So, you are protecting him. You know, maybe he was playing at being old and feeble. Maybe he's the street boss. Maybe he runs all the drugs. Maybe he killed them and set us up to take the fall." She kept looking at his house.

I didn't think her theory had much merit. The cops would go door to door, and he could tell them the same thing he told us, or he could plead ignorance. Whoever committed the murders would have needed stealth, and fast reflexes. No matter how much he was playing up his age, Mr. Ozwald wasn't capable of either of them.

"We came here because of the address I got from Sara," I said. "He just gave us reason to go in. I might have done that the first time anyway."

Now she was starting to bounce on her feet. "But that's not what happened."

I couldn't figure out why she was acting like this. One second she had my back, now she was preparing to run. "I don't want him to get hurt." I didn't need to look over my shoulder at the other houses. The sirens would bring people to see the action. If I stayed and spoke to the cops, there'd be no reason to suspect Mr. Ozwald of making the call.

"You care more about a man you just met than you do about me or Lu."

"That's not true." I had offered to let her leave after all.

"You won't help either of us with our problems, but you'll lie to the cops for him." Her eyes were blazing now. What had started as an attempt to shield her from the cops, escalated to a fight in less than sixty seconds.

"I don't know how to help you or Lu. This is what I do, Val." I knew the argument wouldn't work. Something had gotten to Val's fears; logic wouldn't even touch the problem.

"Fine. Do what you have to do. When I was on the street, if you lied to the cops, things always got worse." She was looking around like a trapped cat. "You're going to lie; not a little one about the door, but a big one. Something that might get in the way of catching the killer. You won't get a lawyer, and you'll end up hurt. This time I'm not going to watch."

Before I could say anything, Val ran for the corner, turning just as a police cruiser came speeding into the street a block away. I stopped watching her. If she was lucky, Val would have been out of sight by the time the cops looked. They pulled over, blocking the street, and the passenger got out yelling at me to put my hands up.

I obeyed, relieved that they hadn't noticed Val.

TWENTY-NINE

It wasn't as simple as I hoped.

Rather than question me on site, the cops had put me in the back of their cruiser while they taped off the house and garden. The detectives showed up about five minutes after the cruiser, and they went into the house. I didn't see them again, but someone must have vouched for me because the car door opened and I was told to go to the Main Street station and wait to be interviewed.

Great. At least, I wouldn't have to come back for my car, and I wouldn't have to wait for lunch until after the interview. I didn't have to go straight to the station; no one would be there for a while, but I kind of did have to. If I jerked them around, the next time the cops had me in their custody, they wouldn't be so trusting.

So, I stopped at a Wendy's on the way, ate a quick burger and fries, and then made my way back across town to the police station. I lucked out again and got parking within a block. It was lucky more than just for the location. As soon as I put the car in park and turned off the engine, the shakes started. I'd been so busy focused on Val, on the cops, on getting food, on getting here, that my body hadn't had time to react properly to seeing the corpses.

It's not like I haven't seen them before, but it never got easy. I knew there was no point trying to control the reaction, so I sat in the car, breathing, and letting my body deal with the adrenalin and grief. Yeah, I didn't know the junkies, and I barely knew Iain, but I had to deal with the loss. Maybe some guilt too. If I'd been more professional, maybe Iain wouldn't have lied.

When the shakes subsided, I wiped my eyes, and checked that I didn't look a total wreck before going into the cop station. I didn't want anyone thinking I was a victim of some sort when I walked through the door.

On the way to the building, I called Val. Voicemail. Maybe she was still mad at me. "You are off the hook, I think. At least until they talk to Mr. Ozwald and find out I wasn't alone. I'll try to deal with it for you. I'm going into the station now. I'll call you when I get out."

She could act like a child, at least for another few years; I was an adult, and I think I just proved I could actually act like one occasionally.

I checked in at the front desk and then sat on one of the vinyl waiting chairs. They were locked together in a row and bolted to the wall. Maybe people stole them if they weren't tied down. I wasn't alone. There were five other people waiting. A mother with two kids in diapers. She looked run down from more than just the kids. I think she was too familiar with this part of the police station. There were two bikers sitting at the other end of the row; one had a black eye, and the other kept patting his pocket, like he was missing a gun, or a knife.

My phone rang: Lu.

Catching the eye of the guy at the desk I made sure he knew I was going outside. There was no reason to take the call in the waiting area. When someone was ready to take my statement,

I'd hang up. No way was I going to lose the privilege of being allowed to leave a crime scene.

"Hey," I said as I walked through the door to the street.

"Are you okay?" Lu sounded out of breath, like she'd run to make the call, or was really scared for me.

"I'm fine." I gave her a quick rundown of the facts. "Still no dog, but I guess that case is probably closed."

"And Val? Is she still with you?"

"No. Listen, I don't have much time, what did you call me for?"

"I can't call out of concern for my friend who keeps stumbling over dead bodies?"

I snorted a laugh despite the remnants of shock in my system. "I didn't fall this time."

"I called because I screwed up and don't know what to do. And I'm freaking out because I'm freaking out." Lu's voice went from joking to panic in the space of two sentences.

"What did you do?" I had my suspicions but didn't want to jump in blind.

"The wedding. I forgot about all the details I need to deal with. When I said that we'd have a big wedding and we'd hire a planner, I forgot she'd need me to have some idea for the ceremony, the flowers, the dress, everything." She gulped in a breath and started talking again.

I let her run out of steam because she wouldn't be able to listen until she got it all out. Her panic made me doubly glad that Jake and I had a long-distance relationship. Every time we talked or got together, it was about the moment, not the future.

"... And Matthieu keeps saying 'whatever you want is fine with me'." She took another breath and it was my turn to talk.

"Oh, what a tangled web —."

"Shut up. I know I screwed up. Tell me how to fix it." There was no humor left in her voice.

"Fine. You need to tell Matthieu the truth. You need to figure out between you exactly what is going to happen on the day."

"Like it's that easy."

"It is easy. Lu, you need to grow up." I knew as soon as the words were out that it was the completely wrong thing to say, and I didn't really mean it. But I'm in the middle of a case that turned up multiple bodies. I can't always be responsible for my mouth. And Lu would know that.

"I can't believe you told me that." I could hear the stress tighten her voice.

Now I felt guilty rather than just justifying my bad behavior. "I'm sorry."

"I'm always there for you," Lu said, drowning out my apology.

And she was right. Lu was the one I always relied on to bring me back to earth. Being on the other side of the problem wasn't fun and, clearly, I wasn't good at it. I had no other advice. Jake and I might not see each other much, but we didn't play games. Neither did Lu until now; did that mean there were deeper problems than just a ceremony? I wasn't opening that topic when she was in stage three panic.

I could only offer one thing again. "Lu, I said I was sorry. Look, you have to figure out why it's a problem. Why you keep trying to make it perfect for each other without talking it through."

Someone tapped me on the shoulder. Leigh Andrews, my best cop friend.

"Lu, I have to go. I'll call you when the interview is done."

I didn't wait for her to start the next outburst.

THIRTY

I followed Leigh into an interview room.

"I need you to leave your phone on my desk." Leigh held out her hand.

This wasn't normal, but I wanted to get this over with. There were a few people I needed to contact before the cops got to them. So, I handed over my phone and watched her put it in the top right-hand drawer of her desk.

"If you want to see me, Charity, you could ask me out for coffee," Leigh said.

She was usually all business.

"This is more fun, though." I hesitated to ask about her mood, none of my business.

"So, three bodies this time." She pushed a pad of paper toward me. "You can write out your statement here."

This was weird. "Don't you want to hear it?"

Leigh grinned and tidied two file folders she'd brought with her. "It's refreshing to have you volunteer information."

"So, your sweet and nice cop act was just to put me off kilter?" I laughed; Leigh knew me better than that. "Let's just get this done."

She leaned forward and glanced at the top corner of the room where a tiny red light betrayed the presence of a camera. "I'm taking an interrogation course. It's rare that I get to try out the more out-there approaches. I knew you wouldn't fall for it."

That's the Leigh I know and... well, like was probably enough. "I went to the house looking for a dog."

"I don't see you as the kind of person who would want a dog. Maybe a cat, or a self-reliant fish."

"It was a case. My neighbor's dog was kidnapped. I was supposed to pay the ransom." It wasn't being obstructive to hold back irrelevant information. If she wanted to practice interrogation tactics, she could figure out what to ask.

"Which neighbor?"

I swallowed a lump of grief before I could speak. Fine, I didn't really know Iain, and what I did know wasn't pleasant. But he was a neighbor and death wasn't easy. "Iain O'Keith. He's one of the bodies."

"If you were going to pay the ransom, what was Mr. O'Keith doing there?"

"We got our wires crossed the day before. I went to the wrong place the first time. Then I got the right address and you know what happened."

She huffed. Now it was impatient cop practice. "Did you find the dog?"

I shook my head. "I'm hoping he'll show up at home. If the other two guys were the dognappers, then Mickey is probably running free."

"Did it seem weird to you that a dognapping would end in murder?" Her fingers were tapping on the files.

"I figure there is more to it, but I haven't a clue."

Leigh relaxed back in the chair. Well, maybe relaxed is the wrong word. The chairs were metal and not really large enough for lounging. "Will they find any of your prints at the house?"

"Probably," I said.

"Anyone else's?"

"Sure, I guess they had visitors."

"I mean was anyone else with you?"

Val had been very careful not to touch anything. Was she talking about hair and fibers?

"No," I said after what I hoped wasn't too long a pause. "I went in alone."

"That wasn't smart, Charity."

Leigh slid the top file toward me flipping it open to the first page. It was a rap sheet and a photo. I'm sure it was one of the dead guys, but I hadn't looked that closely at the corpses.

"Why are you showing me this?"

She pointed to the list of priors. "This guy has been in and out of jail for petty crimes. We think he is behind a spate of pet snatches. We've had ten people complain that they were being extorted for the return of a dog or cat."

"People report this kind of crime?" I wasn't faking it. When Iain asked me to find Mickey, I did wonder if we should call the cops. But they had their hands full with real crime, or so I imagined.

"Yep, and they expect us to do something about it. We're pretty sure that for every one that got reported two or three didn't."

I looked at the other file. "Is that his partner?"

She flipped it open and I saw the other dead guy glaring from a mug shot.

"What made you suspect them?" I asked because I didn't think Leigh would have pulled the file this fast if there wasn't already an investigation going on.

"They were feeding a habit. One of our CIs mentioned that they had dogs with them sometimes, different ones." She pulled the files toward her. "They signed a lease so we ID'd them fast. I guess the pets of Vancouver are safe again."

Great for the dog, but I got the feeling the two junkies weren't killed for taking the wrong dog. And Mr. Ozwald didn't mention any cats. So, the two dead kidnappers might not be the only ones working the scam.

"Any idea who killed them?" I ran the events of the last day through my mind. There was only one oddity and I wouldn't give up Sara right away.

"Your client likely didn't do it," Leigh said. Her expression made me wonder if she was hoping otherwise. But, really? A murder suicide over a pet that went missing?

"I don't know him that well, or I guess I didn't know him. He didn't strike me as the killing type. He had a good job, a new relationship. He hired me to get his dog back, not to find the people who took Mickey and exact revenge."

"We'll follow up on the known associates of our two ransom artists." She looked at the files again and then at the camera. "My gut tells me that they were killed because of your client."

My gut agreed. "What do the detectives think?"

She straightened and tidied the files again. "It's probably too soon. I'm new at the investigative side. You know my back-ground is tactical. All I got from the detectives were orders to ask you what you knew, and advice to keep my ideas to myself."

That must have rankled. It came as a surprise to me that Leigh was looking to advance in the department. She'd have trouble dealing with the politics if she didn't learn to listen first and offer suggestions later. "So, you are sidelined?"

"Not exactly."

I'm not sure why I suddenly felt the need to help her out, maybe because she'd saved my life. Maybe because she gave me some tips now and then, but I knew I wouldn't have helped the detectives the same way. "Iain was having an affair with a married woman. She moved into his place in the last couple of days."

"How do you know?"

"I can't give you anything else, because I have a client involved." I probably could push the line a little further, but I wasn't feeling that generous.

"Did her husband know?"

"I'm not sure." I wouldn't bet that Sara had called her husband by now. And now, I needed to be the one to talk to him first. If the cops just went charging in, I could lose my reputation. "Should I get him to call you?"

Leigh squared her shoulders. "No, you should tell me who he is, and then stay out of it."

"I can't do that, Leigh."

"And what if he's the killer. He'll run."

She had a point, but I wasn't backing down. "I need to close out my case with him. I'll let you do the rest."

"I'll get your phone. You can make the call now, and we can be on our way to him."

THIRTY-ONE

Shit, I should have thought this through when I had my generous urge to help her. "I don't have his contact information on me. I need to get back to my house and pull the file." And I needed to talk to Sara if I could before she heard about Iain on the news.

Leigh leaned in. This time it didn't feel like she was confiding, it was definitely threatening — not that it worked on me. "I could hold you here until you give me the information."

"I'd just call a lawyer." I sat back and crossed my arms.

"That's fine. Your lawyer will tell you to cooperate." Her words were hard, and I knew I was losing any friendly connection that we had.

This was ridiculous. "You know that will just waste time. How about a deal."

She glanced at the camera again. "What do you have in mind?"

This couldn't be on record because it would do Leigh damage when the detectives reviewed the file. I looked at the camera too, then turned back, stared at her, and moved my hand subtly to indicate the door. "You let me go, and I'll come back with my lawyer tomorrow. Maybe he'll agree with you, maybe he'll tell me to take the right to remain silent."

She looked at my hand and nodded. My subtlety had worked. She knew we needed to be off the record. "I guess that's better than waiting all day for your lawyer. If you don't get back to us by nine p.m., there will be officers at your house."

I agreed and she escorted me to the door.

Outside, Leigh stood in my way. "So, what's the real deal, Charity?"

"You want to show you have skills in detection, right?"

She nodded. "I need something to prove myself so I don't get relegated to coffee runs for a year."

"I'll make sure the information comes to you, not the detectives. I'll give you what I can, you use it to prove your worth."

Her eyes narrowed. I didn't have time for her to haggle with me.

"That's the deal, Leigh."

"Okay, deal. When do I get the information?"

She'd never struck me as the ambitious type. There was something going on to make Leigh so hard-nosed. "As soon as I can. I promise I'm not screwing around. I have a couple of things to do first. How long before you have to give up the details about the affair?"

"They'll be back soon. Unless they've suddenly become enlightened about rookies having ideas, I figure they'll call for me in a couple of hours." She took hold of my arm, not hard, but not a gentle friendly grip either. "This is really important to me, Charity. I trust you, but I can't cut you too much slack."

I nodded and released her fingers from my arm. Leigh would trust me for this, and maybe, if I came through, she'd be easier to deal with in the future.

THIRTY-TWO

I got out of the station fast. It was getting late and I had all kinds of suspicions rolling around in my brain. The last thing I needed was to have the detectives on the case come rolling in and decide they would ask me their questions in person.

In my car, I made the call to the number Sara gave me. It rang three times and I was composing a voicemail in my head when she answered.

"Did you find Mickey?"

That was odd. I would have asked about Iain first, but then it's not my relationship. "No, but I have some bad news."

"Tell me." Her tone was demanding, and it seemed to come more naturally to her than the pleading she'd done earlier.

"Did you call your husband?" I wasn't about to let her control the conversation. Matthieu had taught me the value of keeping a suspect off kilter. Now that was interesting. When had I started considering Sara a suspect?

"I was going to do it when he got home from work. It didn't feel like the kind of information he'd want to hear when he was out on a job." She paused long enough that I was about to jump in. "Did something happen to my husband?"

Still not asking about Iain. I felt sorry for him. I figured she was using him as a steppingstone to get away from a marriage she didn't want. "No." I wondered how low Iain was on her list.

"What's the bad news?" Suspicion soured her tone.

"The police will be calling soon," I said. Now was the part that would be tricky. I should let the cops make the notification. They liked to see the raw reaction. But I didn't care for her attitude. Now, I wanted to see her face when I told her. "Are you at Iain's?"

"Yes. I can't go wandering around town until we tell Billy about us." There was a sulk in her voice now.

"I'll be home in twenty minutes. I'll tell you the news in person."

"No. What am I supposed to do until you get here? I'll be a wreck. Tell me now."

I ended the call.

Iain getting murdered was awful, but at least he wasn't around to get hurt by Sara.

Time to get home. I wasn't going to call Billy Lyman from my parking spot, and this wasn't the kind of call you made while driving. I had no idea how he'd react, but the best outcome I could think of was that he'd be relieved. Sara Lyman was never planning to stay with him. He was a plumber, and my guess is her next victim would be a little higher up on the economic ladder than Iain. She only had a few years to be a trophy wife, and then she'd age out.

When I told her twenty minutes, I left out the part about the drive only taking five. After I parked, I went into the Bayshore Hotel and sat in the lounge. It was quiet at this time of day and I wasn't going home until I was ready to speak to Sara. One of the waiters headed in my direction.

"I just need a few minutes," I said.

He went back to the bar.

I dialed the number I had for Billy Lyman. Yes, I know I lied to Leigh, but she made it so easy. And it wasn't beyond the realm of possibility that she'd known I was lying.

"Charity?" Billy Lyman said.

"I have some news for you, Mr. Lyman."

"You found her? Is she okay?"

When it came to missing spouses, I usually got a vibe from the client. Over four of these cases, I'd had two clients who were happy to have their spouse located — both had gone on a revenge vacation after a fight. One had just wanted to find her husband so she could serve him divorce papers. And the other, told me to let them stay where they were. I could tell by his voice that Billy Lyman was one of those who wanted her back no matter what. Hope kind of lifts you up.

"She's fine. What do you want me to do?"

I listened to the silence.

"Do you think she wants to come home?"

No. "I can give you her number. You can call her to find out." If it worked out right, I'd be there when he called. I didn't care for loose ends and, my experience told me that this case was going to have a few.

"That's great, but do you think she's willing to try again?"

Oh, he was still hopeful that his marriage could be saved. Well, he knew her better than I did. Maybe he had a chance.

He wasn't going to let me off the hook, and I needed to get to Sara before she started thinking about other options, and before the cops arrived.

"She moved in with another man."

"So, they are together?"

He'd hear it on the news, but I couldn't have it get back to Sara before I saw her again. "I don't think it's working out."

"Give me the number and send me your bill. Thanks, you did a great job."

I repeated the number for Sara's cell and hung up. I dug a five-dollar bill from my pocket and dropped it on the table. It always helped to keep the staff sweet.

As soon as I left the hotel, I started picturing Sara running right after my call. It's what she did, as far as I could tell; when things got sticky, she ran. So, I made record time getting to the end of my street, expecting to see her getting into a cab and driving away.

Sara opened the door when I walked up. She'd been watching me come down the finger dock.

THIRTY-THREE

If her scowl didn't tip me off to her mood, the crossed arms, and the way she blocked the entire entrance screamed pissed-off. "What's the bad news? I can't wait around any longer, Charity. You owe me a straight answer."

Not sure when we'd racked up that debt. I didn't owe her anything. But arguing about it wouldn't get me answers. "You might want to sit down."

Sara stood aside to let me in then shut the door behind me. "Just tell me, Charity. No more stalling. I can't take the worry anymore." She'd moved from aggressive to concerned in a matter of seconds.

Her phone rang before I could answer.

She looked at the caller ID. "Shit. Did you tell him where I was? Is that the news? That you've told my husband how to find me?"

Again, the words didn't quite match expectations. There was threat rather than fear in her voice.

"I didn't tell your husband where you were, just your phone number."

She tapped the phone and tossed it onto the couch. "I'll talk to him later."

I just laid it out. "Iain has been killed."

She paled, and then flushed with anger. "What about Mickey?"

"Why is the dog so important to you?"

"Not your concern, Charity. Iain's gone, and Mickey is lost. Don't you care about Mickey?" She leaned in, and, even though I was just the little bit taller, I felt intimidation radiate from her.

"Don't you care about Iain?" I asked.

"Fuck you."

That was enough. "I don't think you want to act like that when the cops show up."

"You sent the cops here?" Now she was more than angry with me. There was a growl of threat in her words. "Get out!"

What could I do? I left.

When I got inside my house, I called Leigh and told her to send someone to pick up Sara before she disappeared.

THE COPS BUZZED me to get through the security gate. I let them in and went back to my desk. If they wanted to talk to me, they could knock. I needed to do some paperwork before I lost track of all the things that I'd learned.

First, I closed the Lyman file, sending Billy the invoice for my time — not a lot since I basically stumbled over her while working another case. The only thing outstanding was the missing heir and that was just in a holding pattern. I needed something to fill my time.

I hadn't heard back from Jake, which was unusual, so I sent him a text asking when we could talk. After dealing with Sara's drama, I realized how important Jake was to me. He kept me grounded, and, to be honest, a nicer person than I would be otherwise. What Sara made me realize, now I thought about it, was that he and I were perfect together. Our careers took us away a lot, him geographically, and me emotionally. It worked most of the time, but right now, I wanted to hear his voice. I wanted to let him know what I felt. I really wanted to see him, but there still wasn't enough free time for me to make the trip out to Australia.

I checked my messages. Most of them were spam, a couple were reminders of renewals on the services that I used to get information, and one was an email from someone I didn't know. It's not unusual, my email is on the business card. The spam blocker was good, so it was unlikely to be a problem if I opened it. And the subject line grabbed me by my curiosity.

Think you've solved the case?

I clicked the heading and started to read the contents. There was no signature, and it started with '*don't try to trace me because I have the skills to hide. Don't try to ask me questions, because I won't get involved beyond this*'.

There was no guarantee that it wasn't a nut job, but not everyone wanted contact with the cops. I read on.

The killings were not about the dog. The two idiots didn't do as they were instructed. They got greedy and that was their last mistake. The dog's owner had something of importance and now he's dead.

You need to find what the killer didn't get.

That was it. No indication of what to do with 'it', and no real threat. I couldn't send this to Leigh without a lot more information. I couldn't ignore it because there could be more deaths. If Iain had something, then maybe they'd go after Sara.

I didn't know Iain well, but he'd always seemed a bit of a normal guy. Okay, the Sara thing should have changed that opinion, but what the hell could Iain have that would be important enough to kill for? And where would he have put it?

If Sara left Iain's place, I could search it. It wasn't like he'd died there. The crime scene was across town. The main obstacle I faced was that I wouldn't know when I found 'it'.

THIRTY-FOUR

It was going to be a while before I could get into Iain's house. So, I sat on the couch and relaxed. I needed to let my brain filter the information I had. Maybe my brain could work out what Iain had that was so important.

My phone rang; maybe a new client. One who was alive to pay the bills.

"I called to apologize for yesterday."

Not even a hello, just waited a beat and said the words. Fine, two could play at this game.

"For what?" I thought I recognized the voice but needed confirmation before I decided between hanging up or listening.

"The phone call. I understand that I should have been nicer. I need your help locating something."

He did sound sorry. Maybe he just didn't have the social skills for small talk.

"And who are you?"

"I'll provide that information when we have a deal."

Not *if* we have a deal. I wanted more out of this guy so I knew who I was turning down. "Who gave you my name?"

"I think I need to keep that confidential for now." He didn't wait for me to reply. "Someone stole a valuable piece of equipment from me; it contains information that is vital to my business. I need it back."

I was good at finding things, not so much retrieving information. "I'm not an Intellectual Property specialist."

"Don't try to refer me. I've been assured you are the right person."

Two things were bothering me. First, this guy was an asshole. Everything he said was coated in arrogance and superiority. Like he was saying, *I could do this if I didn't have more important things to do, and anyway, this is what you working people do.* The other thing wasn't so easy. I knew this voice from somewhere other than the phone call. I couldn't pin down the memory. That said, clients didn't always come in nice packages. In fact, most of the time, they held back secrets, they got mad at the messenger, and sometimes they didn't want to pay. I couldn't run my business on nice people.

"Before I agree to help you, I need a contract and a few more details." Maybe I should have phrased that less like I'd given in, but I couldn't think of any other way to get his name.

A short sigh, like he was too busy to answer my questions. "I'll have my business manager sign the contract. You'll sign a non-disclosure agreement. When I'm satisfied that I can trust you, or sue you to the curb, I'll provide details."

"This isn't a negotiation. I get a contract and details, or I can't help you. I don't take cases that might not be legal."

"I don't do handshake business with people who can destroy what I've built. At my level, trust isn't enough."

What the hell? This was the kind of case I would look back on and know I should have hung up. I didn't because I need income. I run a business and I can't live on the money that flows just from people who act normal. "And at my level, trust is more important than any piece of paper. A good lawyer can always find a loophole in a contract."

"And trust is only good until it's violated. Ms. Deacon, I cannot in all conscience allow this theft to be made public. I insist we do it my way. You will be well compensated."

And there it was. He bought people, and that's why he didn't believe in trust. What he forgot is that people who can be bought can always be bought again. Now, I knew it was time to hang up.

"I'm sorry you feel that way, Mr.?" He didn't jump in with a name — another red flag. "I won't be taking your case. I'm sure you'll find someone else to help you out." I tapped the little red circle to get him out of my life, then put my phone on do not disturb just in case he tried to call back.

The cops had been at Iain's for long enough to get whatever Sara had to offer about his life. All I had to do was wait and watch until they left. If they took Sara in, I could pick the lock on Iain's door. If they left her living there, it would be a problem.

I didn't see her being cooperative, so it was likely that she'd be taking a ride in a cruiser.

THIRTY-FIVE

I was wrong. Ten minutes after my call ended, I watched the cops leave alone. I really needed to get inside that house without a fight.

I called Leigh and left a message. Asking her for an update might not work, but not asking didn't get me anything. I made a pot of tea and took it and my phone to the rooftop patio. From there I could see what was going on.

It was nothing like Delores spying on the neighborhood. I was doing surveillance; she was a snoop.

There was no one around. It was a weekday, so most of the boats were in dock. There were a few people wandering along Cardero, the street that ran along the marina. But it was peaceful. The kind of day that reminded me why I lived here. Two blocks from a busy road, three blocks from the entrance to Stanley Park, it was a little sanctuary in a crowded city.

The curtains in Delores' front room moved. I hoped she wasn't planning on coming over and interrogating me about the police visit — interrogating and blaming. There was a nice person inside my neighbor, but she was kept inside by the very judgmental outside person.

My phone rang, giving me a good reason to go inside.

I checked the ID before answering. I wasn't in the mood for my mysterious caller. "Hi, Sara."

"Did you send the police over?"

She was still mad at me. Well, if she thought her private life was her own, she'd be rudely surprised. A murder investigation brought everything to light. "I didn't have a choice. You might know something that can help solve the case."

"I do," she said, her voice suddenly quiet. "At least, I think I do."

I put my tea mug down and pulled a notepad toward me. "Either you do or you don't, Sara. What did the cops think when you told them?"

I could hear her breathing, so I knew she hadn't hung up on me, but the pause was getting too long. "Sara, what did they say?"

"Fine. I didn't tell them, okay? If what I know has nothing to do with the murder, then I'm wrecking Iain's reputation. I told the cops I wanted my lawyer present the next time they talked to me." She wavered between snarly and scared. I guess she hadn't counted on all of these complications when she traded up from Billy the Plumber to Iain the Consultant.

She'd regret acting like a criminal to the cops, but I didn't care. "Are you going to tell me this secret?"

"Maybe." She took a long breath, almost a sigh. "Look, I'm sorry about how I reacted before. I was in shock. My whole life got turned upside down. I had to think what to do."

The apology didn't fool me. Maybe I was jaded about women who ran off from their husbands, but everything Sara said sounded like a lie. "If you aren't going to give me the information, why did you call?"

"To tell you I'm going back to Billy. I don't want to be alone."

Selfish bitch. I guess it was up to Billy to accept that he was just the temporary man in her life. "Okay. But you didn't need to tell me that. My dealings with your husband are over. My job was to find you."

"I know that. Fine. I'll tell you what I know, but then I'm done, don't try to contact me again."

She really did live in a fantasy world. "What is the information?"

"Will you tell the police that I told you? That I held out on them?"

I took a deep breath and tried to clean the anger from my system on the exhale like a yoga teacher told me to do. It didn't work, I just got dizzy. But I'm a professional. If Sara wanted to play games, that was up to her. I'd get the information she had and then decide what to do. "I can't promise anything until you tell me."

"I don't want to be involved. Iain was a mistake. I can see that now. I should never have left Billy. I hate dogs. I hate this tiny house. Things were better for me before."

And there it was, the whiny little princess voice.

"Fine. I'll keep your secret. Tell me, and you're done." I lied. If it was something the cops needed to know, I'd pass it on.

"Iain worked for an important client. We both kind of did, but Iain was the one who met with the guy." I could almost hear her scheming mind deciding what to tell and what to leave out. "Iain took something. He promised me that it would make us money... lots and lots of money. And Iain said the world was better off if we had the information. I don't know what that means."

"What did he take?" I was with Sara on the last part. All I knew was if something worth a lot of money got stolen, it rarely ended up being good no matter who owned it.

"He didn't tell me. He said it was for my protection. He just said it was worth more money that I could imagine."

"Who was the client?"

"No. I'm not taking the chance that he'll know I told you."

If I was facing her, I'd probably get what I needed, but all she had to do was hang up on me and then I'd only have this little bit of information.

"Is there anything else?" I didn't want her leaving a detail out because I let her control the flow of information. She struck me as the type of person who would use the 'you didn't ask' defense.

"That's it. Am I going to be hearing from the cops?"

There wasn't much for me to pass on right now. Iain stole something valuable from a client and no one knows what. Although that wasn't true. "Does this client know this thing is gone?"

"Probably, but I got the feeling it was illegal, and he wouldn't get the police involved."

I could find out who this client was. Iain's company would be scrambling to replace him if the contract was big, so maybe they would talk. "The police will likely contact the real owner of this thing first." That's if I passed on the information. I really wanted to get a bit more on this before I called Leigh.

"He's dangerous. It might be a bad idea to talk to him." Now she sounded genuinely scared. "Don't let him know I told you. He might think I have whatever Iain took."

It was a logical guess. In fact, I was pretty sure she knew more about the whole thing than she was telling. "I'm sure it will be okay."

"I'll be gone in a few minutes. Maybe I should just run so no one can find me."

"It's harder to do that than they make out on TV, or in movies." I knew we were done. She wasn't going to tell me anything more. "Don't you want to know for sure who killed Iain?"

"Like I said," her voice was hard and cold. "Iain was a mistake. Don't call me."

She ended the call. I stood there staring at my screen like an idiot for a minute. The woman was more changeable than Val. Except with Val the moods were all hot and cold. With Sara, I couldn't help thinking everything was an act.

At least I had a clue. I'd find out who this client was, and then get a meeting.

THIRTY-SIX

I didn't think that calling Iain's boss and asking which client he worked for was a good idea. I also didn't know where the cops were in the notification process. If I got ahead of them, they would stop me from going any further. The trick to doing a shadow investigation was not getting noticed until you needed help.

The good news was that MainlineData was a publicly traded company, so there was a possibility I could find the information in their financial disclosure documents.

I opened SEDAR, the disclosure website, and started scrolling through the documents for MainlineData. There were specific items that had to be disclosed, but the requirements didn't state they had to be easily found. I hoped that the contract with Iain's client was large enough to be material and so needed to be reported.

The list of documents was daunting.

My phone started vibrating; somehow it had changed ring modes when I wasn't looking. It was Val, and I answered it even though I should have focused on the corporate documents.

"What's up?"

Please don't ask me to mediate a fight between Val and Rory, I begged the universe.

"I'm sorry about running away." She sounded really down.

"It's okay. I wasn't long and there was nothing to tell them," I said. "I didn't mention you, but Leigh did ask."

"Why?" Panic tightened her voice.

Back on the roller coaster of Val's internal story. "She knows you help me out. Don't worry. Is that why you called?"

Val sighed. "No. Maybe. I think this thing with Rory is making me crazy. I'm going to tell him it's off. I don't have the time, or energy, for his drama." Despite her words, Val sounded far from settled. If pressed, I'd say defeated was close to the truth.

I stifled a laugh; she probably wouldn't appreciate the irony in her current mood. As far as I could see, Rory poured his drama into filmmaking and she did it into everyday life. "If you wait for the time to be right, you'll be a single woman for a long time."

"Well, maybe that's for the best. It's not like I have a great history with guys."

This Val was a stranger. She'd always been cocky, but her bad moods were usually anger fueled. Now she sounded depressed. Like her past as a prostitute was suddenly haunting her. Although, being in love with one of the Rance MacDonalds might be the problem. I didn't think Rory, or his parents would hold her past against her, but maybe social pressure was getting to her.

"Your history is not important, Val. It's what you do now, not what you did to survive before."

Another sigh. "Easy to say, hard to live."

I wasn't making any headway. This subject needed a pizza and a bottle of wine — for me, Val still wasn't quite legal to drink.

"Come over tonight and we'll talk." I was optimistic that I'd have the information I needed soon enough to take the night off.

"Like the old days? Can I have a glass of wine?" Her mood seemed to have bounced up.

"No wine, but yeah, just like the old days. I have to go now, Val."

I held my breath waiting for her to make some snarky remark, but she just said okay, asked me to call her when I was ready, and hung up.

I went back to the computer and found the list of material business relationships. There were three that might fit the bill; DeBerg Corp, Matthews Development, and Wyatt Mining.

I should be able to find the contact information for each of the CEOs, but I wasn't naive enough to think the head of the company would answer the phone. I needed a cover story and a good one, because I intended to get a face-to-face meeting for this afternoon. All three were headquartered downtown, so it was a possibility.

The research had done me a favor, or two, I guess. I got the information I needed, and I got a distraction from the love lives of my two best friends. Now that I wasn't fretting over the case, my mind was free to fret over Val and Lu, and how much I was helping versus how much damage I was doing.

THIRTY-SEVEN

The fastest way to help my friends was to close this case. So, I wrote down the three contact numbers, but before I could come up with my story, my phone rang. It wasn't Val or Lu, so no love guru conversations. It was unknown, but it looked familiar, and not from a common spam area code.

"Yes?" I didn't need to be polite to a machine, and if it was a person, I wasn't exactly being rude, just busy.

"If I tell the police what I saw, you and your little Asian friend will go down for murder."

I held the phone out to make sure I got the number. I made a note of it on a scrap of paper and activated the recording app.

"Who are you?" I didn't expect an answer. I just needed the call to go on more than a second or two. The longer we talk; the more towers would register when I traced the call.

"That's not important." The voice was disguised, and the program switched filters. Fancy, it would be harder to find the real voice on analysis. It sounded male, but that could be part of the alteration.

"What do you think you saw?" The bodies had been dead long enough that it would be a stretch to think Val or I did it. I'd get in trouble for lying about her being there. Not enough trouble to take this call seriously, though.

"You sent her away. Why?"

So, this was going to be a game of questions. "Why did you call?" It would go on as long as one of us held onto information. I'd end the call when I thought I knew enough. He'd end the call if he got frustrated.

"You need to get me what Iain O'Keith stole."

Not stole from me? It might not mean anything, but it was weird.

"What did he steal?"

"If you don't get it back, more people will die."

"Did you kill Iain and the two junkies?"

"No." He said it like I was stupid for thinking that.

"Did you have them killed?" If it was one of the CEOs, they wouldn't get too personal with the murders.

"Stop asking questions. You need to retrieve the USB. You need to contact me at this number when you have it. I will give you instructions from there."

At least I had a new piece of information. "USBs are pretty common. How will I know I have the right one?"

"It has a design on the case; a blue scarab."

"How big is it?"

"The capacity doesn't matter. You can't access the information."

I was getting an idea of the cadence of his speech. This was my mystery caller. Another phone I could track.

"I didn't mean that," I said. "I meant how big is it physically?"

I must have surprised him because there was a long pause.

"If you can't give me more than 'it's a USB'," I said, mimicking the voice distortion. "Then I'm not going to be able to find what you need."

"It's about a half inch long. They are all the same width."

"I knew that." The call was going on longer than I hoped. I'd be able to trace this no problem. Of course, if I wanted to keep everyone safe, I couldn't waste too much time tracking my caller down. I started getting my investigation bag together. "How do you know about me?"

"That doesn't matter."

"It does to me." I jammed my camera and a flashlight into a backpack. Unlike my American counterparts, I had no gun. I knew how to shoot one, but I wouldn't own one. "Someone told you about me." I didn't say, you've known about me since Iain dropped by.

"I have my sources. I checked you out. You have a reputation for being willing to go too far to solve a case. You live next door to the man who stole my property."

"Fair enough." I was ready to go as soon as he hung up. I wasn't going to end the call. If he was feeling chatty, I would prise out any detail I could. "Did you follow me last night?"

"Why would I admit that?"

So, the answer was yes. If he didn't know who followed me, then he'd have said something more on the denial side than the deflect side.

"I just want to make sure no one else is after me. If your competitors want the USB, I'll be fighting them off."

"I have no competitors." Then he ended the call.

THIRTY-EIGHT

I typed the phone number into my semi-legal copy of the tracing software. It took all of three seconds to show me that the calls had bounced off cell towers downtown. It didn't narrow it down at all since the three companies were located within the same square block.

What did help was that the caller had moved from Burrard and Hastings east toward the stadium, and then south. He'd been in a car by the distance he'd gone in that time.

It irked me that I couldn't do anything with the information, and it surprised me that I could get it. What kind of villain doesn't know how to disguise his whereabouts on a phone?

I could try checking the location where the call started. It should tell me which corporation was closest.

No matter what I did to identify the man, I still had to find the USB. There weren't a lot of places I could think to look, but Iain's house would be empty, and that I could go through.

I left the investigation bag on the kitchen counter and tucked my keys and lock picks into my pocket. With my phone in the other pocket, I had everything I needed to get into Iain's place and record what I found.

I glanced at Delores' house before hurrying down to Iain's door. If she saw me, I'd hear about it, but I didn't think Delores would call the cops on me — at least not right away.

The lock was simple enough. I was inside in about the same time as if I'd had a key. Sara hadn't made any impact on the state of the house. I should have kept an eye out for her leaving. My guess was she took a suitcase full of her clothes and just left everything else behind. The cops may have searched, but they would only be looking for a gun if they suspected her of the murders.

The scattered boxes looked much the same. The clothes were in piles on the floor as if Sara had sorted through them for hers and dropped anything she didn't pack. If Iain had the USB it could be anywhere in the mess. I would go through it all if I had to, but first I checked for an office. There was one.

Like most things on a floating home this size, the room was tiny. A desk with drawers on each side sat under a window that looked out into the inlet. Iain could work and stare at mountains, boats, and water for inspiration. Or, at least, could have done that. There was a shelf set into the wall above the desk. That, and a chair was all of the furniture. Going paperless had its benefits when space was scarce.

The desk held a laptop, a coaster for a coffee cup, a mouse, and a keyboard. The USB stuck in the laptop was for Bluetooth connection, not for storage of data. I opened each drawer in turn; there were six altogether. Two were empty; well there was a paper clip stranded in one. Another held peripherals, a lapel microphone, a mouse pad so old it was starting to crumble, a DVD drive and a couple of random cables. From the other three, I took a handful of swag from some kind of conference, a stack of Post-it notes, and a package of whiteboard pens

There were three USBs in the mix. None had a scarab on

the case. Although two of them were novelty; a piece of sushi and a rock climber. I guess he had a whimsical side.

A quick scan of his bedroom didn't show much. His bathroom was small. I looked in the cabinet and saw something that might explain his weird behavior; a pill bottle of Xanax prescribed to a Mrs. Julia Baldwin. I looked inside, only a few small pills remained.

I picked some of Mikey's hair off my pants and went back to the living room. The kitchen took over one wall, a small dining table and four chairs occupied a corner, the rest was the couch that now faced the window, two easy chairs a coffee table, a giant TV, and the aforementioned mess.

It was going to take a long time to sift through everything looking for a small USB. Time I probably didn't have. It wouldn't take too long to do a cursory check though, but I would come back later to do a better search.

One thing caught my eye; a keyring sat in a bowl on the coffee table. I made sure it contained the front door key and then dropped it in my pocket. It would be much easier to explain my presence if I had what looked like legitimate access.

I checked down the side of the couch and chair cushions — I found the remote for the TV. Then I tossed some of the clothes aside. Again nothing. Iain was far better at hiding what he took than he was at finding his dog. My dislike of him grew every time I hit a dead-end. I was in this for Mickey now.

I couldn't stay focused on the search because I wanted to find the caller. So, I locked the door and headed toward downtown. It was only a ten-minute walk, and I'd spend twice that looking for parking if I took the car.

THIRTY-NINE

The address was in one of the Bentall Towers on Burrard Street. A glass and steel structure that sat with its four brothers beside new and old buildings. I strode into the lobby pretending I had real business there. No one cared. I was one of ten or so people looking for the directory. It was in a free-standing marble block. You typed in the business and it told you where to go.

I searched for Matthews Development first, because it was the only one that had an official presence in this tower. Then I looked for Wyatt Mining — no result. DeBerg Corp had an office one floor above Matthews Development. I headed for the elevators and started with Matthews.

My plan was basic. Find out if the head of the company was in and try to talk to him or her. I was pretty good on my feet, so I tried to be confident that I'd be able to get myself out of any trouble I got into.

As the elevator rose, my confidence plummeted. What the hell was I thinking? Was it conceivable that someone in charge of a large corporation would kill three people for some USB? Probably only in fiction, but it's all I had.

The elevator binged, and I stepped out directly into the reception area of MDI. The receptionist was a polished blond woman in her late twenties. She gave the impression of a current and reliable company. Her smile was friendly but not exactly warm. I guessed her job mainly consisted of keeping out anyone who didn't seem to have the money to invest in a big project.

"Hi," I said, smiling in return. "I thought this was Matthews Development."

She nodded. "You are in the right place, we've just re-branded to MDI. It stands for Matthews Development Incorporated. Can I help you?"

Her tone was all question mark. The subtext was; do you have enough money to be here? Are you here to cause problems? Will you make my job harder?

"You can. I need to speak to Orrin Matthews. He's still the CEO, right?" I hoped my subtext was all about being harmless and possibly useful.

"Yes, Mr. Matthews still heads the company, but I'm afraid you can't see him."

That was a bit final. "Do I need an appointment?"

Her smile widened, meant to forestall any conflict. "Yes, but that won't help you right now. He's climbing Kilimanjaro. Out of contact for four days, starting yesterday. I can make an appointment with Ms. Wheeler. She's replacing him while he's away."

If I was right, this was between me and the person who owned the company, not their second in command. "That's okay. I'll come back if I need to see her. You have a great day now."

"You too," she said.

Now we were in that awkward space where I had to wait for

the elevator while she sat behind me. "Can I use the stairs to go to another office?"

She looked sad. This woman was overly empathetic. "Sorry, the stairs are all locked to key cards."

FORTY

I stood at the elevator pretending to check something on my phone. It seemed to take forever. Maybe because the two businesses occupied floors just below the cut off for the express car, so it stopped at most of the floors below. The whole time it felt like I was being watched, but I refused to turn around to meet the receptionist's gaze. When the bing finally announced the car's arrival, a wave of relief cooled me down. I stepped on the empty elevator, held my breath to defeat the overwhelming scent of someone's cologne, and pressed the button for the floor above. I guess not everyone understood no-fragrance policies.

The DeBerg Corp floor was more conservatively decorated. There was a large walnut door to the business. So anyone visiting had the chance to do a final check of professionalism before entering, without being observed. I gave my skirt a tug and ran my tongue over my lips. One other door led to what was identified as an emergency exit. There were no cameras that I could see, and the door looked pretty much like any other; more solid, and bigger, sure, but it still had one lock and swung on hinges. I can't remember when I first started automatically scoping out the ease of entry for every place I went, but now it was like breathing.

I pushed open the door and stepped inside. This time the receptionist was a man. In his late fifties by the wrinkles around his blue eyes. He wore a dark blue suit with a pale blue shirt, and a dark blue tie. Almost the corporate colors of DeBerg. He looked up and smiled at me with insincere sincerity.

I didn't give him a chance to start his spiel. "Hi. I'm Charity Deacon, I need to see Mr. Bergeron."

"May I see some identification, please?"

It took me a second to realize he was serious. What happened to 'he's not available', or 'I can make an appointment for you in three months'?

"Why do you want to see that?" I was digging in my bag for my wallet where I kept my PI license.

"Is there some reason you don't want to show me?" He didn't make a move to call security, just smiled and waited for me to answer. This was a game to him.

"Is Mr. Bergeron in?" I handed him my license as I asked.

"He is not." The guy pulled out his phone and took a picture of my license. "Please wait here for a moment." He stood to leave, and I didn't know if he was coming back.

"Wait, I need that." I pointed at the license he still held.

"In one moment." He strode down a corridor to his right.

I was tempted to run after him and demand my ID back but thought better of it. I wouldn't leave without it, though. I was sure they wouldn't cause a scene just to keep something they had a picture of, and I was certain this wasn't how DeBerg Corp usually did business. If their clients had money, which the décor and address shouted that they did, there was no way they'd put up with such terse service.

There were no seats in the small area, so I was stuck standing until Mr. Reception came back. It took all of five minutes, giving me plenty of time to check for cameras. There were none inside. When he did return, he was carrying a stiff white envelope, the kind that held greeting cards, or thank-you cards, or invitations you wanted to decline, but couldn't.

"Here's your license."

I took it and tucked it safely back into my wallet.

"I have been instructed to give you this." He handed me the envelope.

"By who?"

His smile widened, and I expected some version of 'I'm not at liberty to say'.

"Mr. Bergeron. Although he said it was from an acquaintance who wished to remain anonymous."

Again, weird phrasing. "I would still like to talk to Mr. Bergeron," I said.

"He left on a business trip. Perhaps I can fit you in for his return?" He glanced at the screen in front of him. "He has an opening in three weeks at six a.m.?"

"I'll have to check my calendar." I wasn't going to open the envelope here. I didn't want this front guy to pass on my reaction to whatever was inside it to his boss. "Do you have a direct line?"

He handed me a business card. "I will hold the spot for a few days. Just let me know."

I was down on the ground floor in less time than it took to get the elevator between floors. I didn't really want to open the message here, in public, but my curiosity wouldn't let me wait.

There was a foil seal on the back. I popped that off and pulled out an embossed card.

Well done. You passed the first test. Now find my USB before I have to take dire steps.

FORTY-ONE

I was out of ideas. I couldn't tell the cops what happened because there was nothing I could give as proof. I knew it was real, but how would I explain the missing dog, the ransom? The chunk of Mickey I found with his collar? In my head, all of this added up to a crime, but would Leigh see it that way?

Whoever this was, and maybe it was this Bergeron character, or someone who was pretending to be him, knew my schedule. That thought triggered a sinking feeling and a memory of the pain after the beating I'd received a couple of years ago.

I hadn't told anyone, other than people I trusted, that I was going on that stakeout, and yet, this guy had been there and followed me afterward. That was the thing that gave me the creeps. Anyone could get my phone number. It was on all of my business cards. I didn't advertise my address unless I had to, because I didn't want people taking out their frustration on me like the first time I investigated a case. Even so there were a few places it could be found. And if this guy knew about Iain, he knew where Iain lived.

If I was going to be spinning in circles, I'd be better off in my own house, so I put on some speed. Maybe inspiration would hit when I didn't feel so exposed. All I could think of right now was searching Iain's place of work. I was pretty sure the killer would have looked there. And that Iain would have found some place less obvious than his office. Or his home.

I noticed my hand shaking as I made sure the security gate was closed tight behind me. I ran down the dock to my house; suddenly afraid it had been trashed again.

There was no sign of a break-in at the door. I opened the door and the reassuring beep of the alarm calmed me down almost back to my normal level of anxiety, which was none. I entered my code and locked the door behind me.

Panic wasn't my usual reaction to threats, but this time it just all felt a little too psychopathic. This was the kind of situation where I needed Jake to be home. He'd yell at me for getting into a dangerous situation. He'd tell me I should bring in Matthieu and the cops. But then he'd hug me, and I'd be ready for the fight.

I pulled out my phone. If I couldn't have the real thing, a text would be almost as good. Except I couldn't let him know the situation. It would be unfair to dump that on him when he was half a world away.

Missing you. When can we talk next?

It was early in the morning, tomorrow in Sidney; well, for actors it was early. Maybe he was up having breakfast, or waiting between scenes, and would see the text right away.

He didn't respond immediately so I put on the kettle to make tea. I could do some brainstorming while I waited.

Can you be up tonight? I mean my tonight?

I smiled at the text. It was almost like him being there. If he called when he didn't have to be on set, we could talk for as long as we wanted.

What time? I added a heart emoticon.

Nine? My nine?

So, my 4 am. I sent him a thumbs up emoticon. Tea in hand, anticipation of my call with Jake in my mind, I sat at the table with a blank sheet of paper in front of me. Where would I hide a USB?

FORTY-TWO

It sounded like a good plan when I thought it up but sitting there looking at a blank page with a question on it didn't raise my investigative muse. I made a list of the places I knew Iain frequented. Then crossed them off as I decided they were unlikely locations for a USB stash; the dog daycare, the dog park, and the coffee shop where I used to see him with Mickey on weekends. The list was short to start with — maybe I should make more of an effort to get to know my neighbors — and now all that was left was his office and his house.

I could spend some time going through all the mess on his floor, and I knew where to look for some hidden compartments. A small floating home often had cabinets in the most unusual places. My office files were tucked into shallow spaces inside the wall of my living room.

This time I'd go prepared. Latex gloves, my camera, a multi-tool, and a few evidence bags that Leigh had given me on a case a while back. If I found anything that would help the cops, I could protect it from contamination. Chain of custody was their problem.

I grabbed the key to his place, doubly glad I'd taken it. If the cops showed up, I could claim Iain had given it to me.

When I was ready, I marched up to Iain's door like I had every right to walk in. I'd learned long ago that attitude covered a lot of sins. Inside, nothing had changed. I hadn't expected anything, to be honest, but if the cops had come to search the house, they might still be inside. My trip downtown hadn't been long enough for them to come and go. But if they had come, they hadn't left anyone on guard, and surely some lowly constable would be stationed at the door.

I checked my phone before I dug into the search for good. It was charged and on vibrate. I left it in my pocket and hung my jacket on a hook beside the door. I needed to be agile, I didn't need to be wondering where I'd dropped the phone if I had to grab and run for some reason.

Still reluctant to go through the clothes, I decided to search for hidden compartments. Along with the file storage, I had two other places in my house. A hidden trap door that went to the crawlspace between the floats and the floor, and a set of drawers that formed the risers on my stairs. Unlike me, Jake had opted for open space rather than secret caches. He didn't collect things and didn't need the room for storage. Iain's was some-where between us. His first floor was fairly open, but his bedroom and office were perfect places to hide a cupboard or drawer.

I started on the top floor. His bedroom walls were all solid. His bed sat directly on the floor and was too heavy for me to lift alone. I knocked on all the walls in the bathroom and found a hidden space in the bath surround. I got down on the floor and reached into the darkness, hoping no spiders lived there. All I got were dirty fingers and a few random dust-covered tools. By the amount of dirt, they must have belonged to the previous owner, and Iain didn't — hadn't — even known they were there.

I tapped the ceiling; no hollow sounds.

Then a buzzing caught my attention. My phone.

By the time I got down to where I'd left my jacket, the call had switched to voicemail. I checked the missed call; Val. Whatever she had to say could wait. I'd check it before I left.

The only thing remaining for me to do was go through the piles of clothes and other debris scattered around the floor. I didn't know who'd come to settle Iain's estate. I had no idea if he had family, that was up to the police. I thought about how that person would feel if they came into the room and had to deal with the mess. I couldn't let that happen.

As I went through each item that I picked up, I folded it, or closed it, or otherwise tried to make it look better. The clothes I stacked on the couch, the books on the kitchen table, and the other items, including a bunch of leashes and collars that must have been Mickey's went on the counter. When I was done, the house looked more inhabitable. Unfortunately, I didn't have a USB. In fact, I was beginning to wonder why anyone would put vital information on a flash drive. There must be ways to keep it in a cloud and still apply security.

I gathered my things and left Iain's house, locking the door behind me. I kept hold of the key, just in case.

FORTY-THREE

When I was home with a bottle of beer and ham sandwich in front of me, I listened to Val's voicemail.

"I'm sorry about being a selfish bitch. You have more important things to do than make sure I don't screw up my life."

Did she really not understand what that kind of message sounded like? A picture of Val running back to her old life at best, or ending it all at worst, blossomed in my head and I couldn't let it go.

I hit call back and waited while the network found her phone and made the connection. You know that space in time where you're not sure you hit dial? It felt like two hours.

She didn't answer. I got her voicemail. It didn't help.

"Val, call me back. I don't know what you are doing, but I'm not going to sit by and let you make a mistake. I'm sorry I've been so busy. Please call me back."

I ended the call because I could feel a babbling coming on, and a tear-filled one at that. I knew in the logical part of my brain, that Val was a survivor, and the message wasn't a cry for help. But in that ancient part of my mind that stirs up all the worst-case scenarios, I knew that Val needed strong support to stay that way.

Now I had a killer who thought I knew something pushing me and a fear of what Val was doing pulling at me.

Fuck it!

The killer could call me no matter where I was. If I went to Val's, maybe I could make sure she wasn't doing something irrevocable.

I took my car. Parking a block away from Val's home, I ran the rest of the way and started banging on her door.

She didn't open it, or yell at me to stop, or anything. I prepared my apology as I used the emergency key she'd given me. If she was inside and not answering, we'd have a huge fight. If she was hurt, I could help. If she was...I couldn't think about that.

The apartment was empty. I had to put my hand on the wall to get my equilibrium back. The rush of adrenaline from panic was still swirling in my bloodstream even though there was no sign of a fight, or a dead body. I couldn't take in any details for a few minutes as I gained control again.

When I was able to focus, I saw a stack of invoices on the coffee table. Then I noticed her calendar open beside it. I felt a warm flush of pride that she'd taken my advice and kept a record of her time in the organizer. That way she didn't have to wing it when she billed people.

I felt guilty and creepy as I took a look in the calendar. Today she had four appointments. One of which was right now. I finally started to believe she was okay. No matter what my ancient brain clamored, Val would never leave a client hanging.

Now all I felt was foolish.

I left. When the door was locked, I looked around to see if any of her neighbors were witnessing my exit. If no one saw me,

Val would never know I'd been there. Then we wouldn't have to have a fight about it.

I promised myself that I would stop pushing her away when she wanted to talk about Rory. If I was her friend, I should listen no matter what she needed to say.

We had plenty of stupid things to fight about, we didn't need her love life as fuel.

FORTY-FOUR

Even though I had nothing to follow in the way of clues, I couldn't settle and wait for the next threat. It wouldn't matter when the killer contacted me. If I didn't have the USB, I wouldn't be able to hand it over. Iain's office still wasn't an option until after normal work hours; too many people around made it hard to get away with snooping. Dressing as a cleaner would get me in when they were closed and that would give me enough time to be thorough without an elaborate cover story.

So, instead of worrying about where to search next, I decided to try to gather enough information to hand this off to the cops. What I had was a couple of phone calls. And some connection to DeBerg Corp. And the car that followed me, which I'm sure got switched for another as soon as the driver realize he'd lost me, and nothing else.

I put myself in Leigh's shoes. She was definitely worried about something, and that meant she'd be unlikely to jump on vague clues. And I valued her as a... friend? Well, more honestly, as a connection to the police, but I felt a bit mercenary confessing that.

Thinking it out wasn't helping me. Everything I tried was a

dead-end. I needed action. If Iain had tried to hide the USB somewhere off site, there were only a few options. The coffee shop was where I saw him the most, but that would be thoroughly cleaned every day and there wasn't likely a place where he could stash something and not have it found.

The dog park was just as unlikely, but there were a few places something might be hidden. There had been a craze for geocaching not that long ago. Lu and I had spent an afternoon following clues until we got bored and went to a bar. One of the common caches was a fake bolt head on a bench. If Iain knew about them, maybe I'd get lucky.

I grabbed my phone and the investigation bag and headed for the park, basically two blocks away. If I found the USB, I would call the number and get this over with, and I'd also have enough to bring in the cops.

THERE WERE ONLY two dogs in the park, so it wasn't that hard to walk in and check the one and only bench. Two owners glanced my way and then got back to their conversation. The bench was made of wooden slats attached by big bolts to a concrete base. The lowest cost for the city, I guess. Before I started touching anything, I did a walk around. None of the bolts looked different from the others. None of the slats had been cut out, at least the visible parts. I didn't see Iain getting on his hands and knees to hide something under the seat. I sat and ran my gloved fingers along the underside of the front, but there was nothing.

It was discouraging, and I was starting to get more attention from the two owners. They probably thought I was dealing or buying drugs. I smiled at them and gave a little wave to disarm them. The only thing left to do was actually test each bolt. I tried to banish the image of multiple layers of dog pee on them, telling myself the bench was hosed down every night. While it didn't look like one of them had been capped with a small container, it would be easy to use the hole meant for the screw part as a hide. In turn, I grasped and tried to remove each bolt. Nothing.

And now the dog owners were on their way over to me. I guess they thought I might be a threat to their precious animals. Waving, I marched past them and headed home.

THE SECURITY GATE clanged shut behind me. I gave it a bit of a shake to make sure the lock caught. That was becoming a habit and I needed to start trusting the gate. It's not like more than one person had violated the security of our little community. I needed to shake the memory of Peter Wong's fist so I could stop waiting for the next beating.

As I turned away, my phone rang. I hated taking the call while I walked to my house; too many people could hear me talk, but it was the unknown caller.

"What do you want?" He needed something from me, and I didn't need his repeat business. So, I could be as rude as I liked.

"Have you got it?"

I opened my door before answering; partly to give me time to think of what to say, and partly to piss him off a little.

"I won't tell you that."

"Afraid I'll come after you?"

At least he wasn't stupid; that boded well for me surviving this encounter. Hopefully more than surviving, it would be nice not to get beaten up, or almost murdered.

"Is that why you called?"

"No. I'll be waiting for you to deliver my data. When you have it, come to the same place you were taking pictures. I expect you before midnight."

"Are you going to be there now?" It was too good an opportunity to get him caught. If he waited, I could send Leigh around.

"Don't bother calling the police. They won't find me. You come as soon as you have the USB. Come alone."

He disconnected.

Come alone. Like I'd bring someone into the situation; someone I'd have to worry about. Of course, the cops could take care of themselves. I'd call and make the arrangements as soon as I knew what I was going to do. Maybe showing up with a USB was all that I needed. He wouldn't know it was a fake until it was too late.

If I got desperate, I'd do just that.

In the meantime, I was going to have to brave Iain's office.

FORTY-FIVE

I called MainlineData, hoping to get a hint about when people left the office so I could slip in as early as possible. The gate-keeper didn't answer. Instead I got a recorded message that MainlineData's offices were closed early for the day and would be reopening in the morning.

That probably meant they'd been informed of Iain's death. Did it also mean the police were on site? There was only one way to find out. I decided to take my car this time. If I found the USB, I could go straight to the drop off, calling Leigh from the car.

I stuffed an overall into my bag, it would pass for a disguise, then I changed into a more businesslike pants and jacket. It gave me options either way. And a security guard might be more forthcoming to a stressed-out woman in a business suit.

There was public parking in the building. I paid less for a week at the Bayshore than I would pay here for a couple of hours, but with luck it would be worth the investment.

I held my phone to my ear as I scurried into the lobby. Giving a loud sigh, I looked around and caught the eye of the uniformed man sitting behind a curved information booth. He was in his fifties, a little overweight, short military haircut, and a bored look on his face.

I straightened my jacket, pasted on a smile, and gave silent thanks to Jake's efforts at improving my acting.

"Excuse me," I said in a strained voice. "I'm trying to reach someone in MainlineData. Do you know why they are closed?"

"I do," he said. So, he had a sense of humor, or no sense of humor and just did everything literally.

"Will they really be reopening tomorrow?"

"That's what they say."

It was less of an effort now to pretend to be annoyed. "Look, I had an appointment with them. A really important one."

"Sorry they can't make it."

"Maybe we can start again," I said. This time I smoothed my jacket and really smiled. "I need to know why they are closed. It's important to my investors. Will you tell me what you know?"

"I don't gossip about tenants. All I can say is the police came and then everyone left. The cops left a half hour ago. Now, I suggest you talk to them tomorrow."

I completed the scene with a sigh and a terse thank you.

I RETURNED TO MY CAR, tossed the jacket and heels into the trunk, pulled on my overall and sneakers and headed for the elevator. I had to count on the fact that they couldn't lock the elevator early — and that I'd be able to get through the door. The actual cleaners would likely come from the freight elevator. I didn't see any way to get there from the parking lot, although it might only go to the ground floor. It might not open up inside MainlineData's office door, and it would definitely require some kind of security pass. I was going to take my chances with one door to break and enter.

I kept my head down when I entered the elevator; it would have some kind of surveillance and I didn't want to make it easy to identify me later. It took me to the main floor, and I had to walk to another bank of elevators to continue. This was going to be tricky since I'd be in full view of the guard. I slumped my shoulders a little and watched my feet as I crossed the lobby. It was hard to control my impulse to hurry, and also to keep from looking to see if I'd been noticed, but I made it into the elevator with three other people.

I waited until the others had punched the button for their floor; then made my selection. It was a good way to see if I'd have company. My luck held out, and I was alone at the stop.

And that's where my luck ran out. The door was locked.

FORTY-SIX

The only good thing about it was that I couldn't see anyone through the all-glass wall that faced the elevator. Of course, that meant I would be seen when I got inside.

I noticed the telltale shine of a camera's red light above the door. Even if I could fool the card-swipe lock, I wouldn't be able to hide my presence, and maybe that camera was a live feed to my humorless buddy on the main floor.

The only option I could think of was to turn left and see if there was another way inside. I refused to let it affect me. Not every break and enter was going to be simple.

I walked the short corridor that led to a set of washrooms. Just past them was one single door. There were no other businesses on the floor, so, if my sense of direction was working, it led to the back of the office. Maybe a lunchroom exit near the toilets? I reached to turn the handle and gave it a twist; locked.

It didn't stall me. I knew it would be easy to pick, and I hadn't seen any sign of a camera in the hall. My hopes were up.

I reached for my phone and put it on do not disturb. The last thing I needed was my phone ringing when I was trying to sneak around.

I pulled my picks out and leaned in to hear what was going on in there — silence. It took ten seconds for me to open the lock and slip inside. Why did people forget the back door when they secured their location? If I was designing the security for this office, I'd have a sensor on all the doors, no matter where they led, and all of the locks would be hard to pick.

The lights were on inside the office, but all I could hear was the buzz of electronics.

Empty offices gave me the creeps. Like the place was haunted by everyone who'd ever worked there.

I hurried through the open space glancing at the cubicles. Each had a nameplate stuck to the fabric wall, it would be easy to find Iain's with that. At least I thought it would be until I noticed the Mickey Mouse nameplate, and the He-man Master of the Universe one. Iain hadn't struck me as the humorous type, so I hoped he'd managed to keep his name real.

I found his cube, in the far corner, of course; making me risk discovery as I tried to use the cubicles as cover for my movements. His cube had a window that faced into the next building. That's one of the benefits of working from my home; my view was of boats and mountains and water. I couldn't throw the feeling that I was being watched from an office across the way. The fact that I couldn't see through that window didn't help me feel confident that I was invisible to anyone there.

The cubicle was spare so searching took all of five minutes — including patting down all of the soft surfaces in case there was a stash in there. I found nothing.

I sat in his chair and started looking for a calendar or diary, or anything that wasn't on his computer — which had resisted my feeble efforts of bypassing the security. If I couldn't find the USB in his home or office, I'd have to learn more about Iain to find out his passwords. There had to be someone he trusted, or a safe place he kept things. A safe deposit box was the logical next step, but I had no idea where he banked, and I hadn't found a key.

Staring at the beige fabric wall of Iain's cubicle didn't spark any ideas. Did the designers pick the color to reduce the chance of independent thought? If so, good job!

The longer I stayed, the more likely I'd get caught. I made my way back to the lunchroom door, glancing at the workspaces as I passed, hoping for a random clue or at least a spark to hit me — more nothing. Outside in the hall, I made sure the door was locked and then ran to the elevator.

Inside and feeling safe, I pulled my phone out and turned it back onto 'disturb'. The first thing was a notice that told me I had no service. I kept the phone in my hands so I'd remember to check for messages. If the killer called, I didn't want to miss it because I got distracted and didn't check.

ON THE MAIN FLOOR, I stayed in the elevator lobby, out of sight of the guard so I didn't have to wait until I got out of the parking lot. A below-ground level was unlikely to have any service.

I kept my eye on the people walking through, but no one seemed to notice me at all.

There was one missed call from Lu and a message.

"Charity, sorry I missed you. Look I'm going to take a few days away with Matthieu. We think it will be easier to talk without distractions. I won't be taking calls. Neither will Matthieu, I hope that doesn't mess up your work, but we have to do this. Bye." It was all rushed and even if I'd answered, I'm sure she wouldn't have let me get a word in.

It was a good idea for Matthieu and Lu to get away from all

the pressure. Maybe they'd have some time to be honest with each other.

I was a little ashamed of the feeling that overrode that rationale. With them out of communication, I was off the hook for supporting one relationship problem for a few days.

FORTY-SEVEN

On the walk to my car I was distracted, and that's my excuse for not noticing the man hanging out until it was too late. He was dressed in dirty jeans and a dark gray hoodie. He leaned against the post two spots away from my car. He straightened as I got closer, drawing my attention.

I pretended not to feel threatened. I could take care of myself, and he was just one person. The little voice inside me wasn't having it. He was stronger than me, and I wasn't much of a fighter.

My casual ignoring didn't work. He walked toward me with a gait that belied his homeless look. Most of the homeless people I'd met tended to shuffle from pain, or just plain hopelessness. This guy swaggered with confidence.

I didn't have anything on me that would work as a weapon, but I could run — not to the elevator, that was how killers and vampires trapped stupid girls in horror movies. I would run for the exit ramp. He was between me and escape, but I could move fast enough that he'd be surprised. I just had to be sure he couldn't grab me.

He stopped just beyond arm's reach. The feeling of being in

danger didn't leave me, but my urge to run quieted. Maybe I was being paranoid and stereotyping him as trouble because he was out of place.

"You aren't getting anywhere looking here," he said. His voice was like a badly auto-tuned recording. I could see the top edge of a band around his neck; a voice distorter.

"Are you following me? I thought I had until tonight." I was proud of my self-control, no quaver in my voice; although it was a lot higher than normal, and it was a bit difficult to get the breath I needed.

He didn't react.

I swallowed to get control of my voice. "If you know where it isn't, then why don't you tell me?"

"You don't seem to be properly motivated." He looked over his shoulder at the sound of a car coming. Then he stepped into the shadow of the pole. Still close enough to grab me if he leaned a little toward me, but less likely to be seen. "I thought you might need a bit more incentive."

"No. Just need to get on with it." I knew the incentive wouldn't be a cash bonus. The usual next step was threatening my friends. "If you don't have any information, let me go back to work."

He chuckled. It wasn't a nice sound. "In my experience, people get more creative if the stakes get personal."

My sense of self-preservation took a second place to my anger. "Look. You have something to say, obviously. Just get it over with and we can both get back to what we do best. I can keep searching for the USB, and you can go back to building your evil lair on some extinct volcano in the middle of the ocean." My mouth wasn't good with bullies.

"Funny." He lurched away from the shadows. "If you don't have what I want by the deadline, your life will start to fall apart. I'll make sure your past is twisted so far that people see you as a thief and liar. I'll change your credit; I'll change the ownership of your house. I'll poison everything you hold dear."

Well it was better than 'I'll kill your friends'.

"Whatever. Are you done?" I took a half step toward him. If I could see under the hoodie, maybe I could pick him out of a mug shot book.

"Just do what you agreed."

He didn't wait for me to say anything else. Just started walking away. I grabbed my phone to get a picture, but by the time I entered my password and found the camera app, he was gone.

It wasn't all that bad. I had something to give Leigh, even if the description wasn't great. Although, bringing in the police now would keep me from finding the USB. Maybe I'd wait until it was time to meet him again. Then, no question, I'd bring in all the help I could get.

FORTY-EIGHT

With no other leads, I went home to try finding more information about Iain. Maybe he had a social media account that would point me in the next direction.

Coffee in hand and laptop open, I took a moment to leave a message for Lu letting her know that she'd done the right thing. I tried to call Val but got her voicemail as well. I didn't bother leaving a message there.

I had Iain's Facebook page open. His settings were pretty loose so there was hope. Of course, there was no banking information, but he'd liked a few financial pages, maybe because he dealt there.

Someone knocked on my door just as I started to click through the list to find his actual friends rather than just people he'd okayed.

It could be anyone — except Val who wouldn't have knocked — but a shock of fear chilled me that it was the killer. It wouldn't be the first time that a threat came from a case. I grabbed the baseball bat that I keep close for emergencies and looked through the peephole.

Not the killer. Delores.

I placed the bat back into its umbrella holder and opened the door. It wasn't just Delores — Mickey sat beside her panting away.

"You found him!" I patted my leg to get Mickey to come. "Delores, that's great."

She looked behind me as if she could assess my validity as a pet sitter by the state of my house. I knew inside she had this rebellious nature and a kind heart. She'd helped me when I was beaten up and came home to find my house ransacked. She'd eventually warmed up to Val, especially since Val treated her with respect. I just couldn't understand why she kept that nice person buried under this judgmental shell.

"It was more like he found me," she said. "I came home from grocery shopping, and he was sitting at the gate waiting to be let in."

I stepped aside to let them enter. "You heard about Iain?" She wouldn't have brought Mickey to me if she hadn't.

"A pity. He liked to keep to himself, but he didn't cause any problems. A good neighbor." She sat at the kitchen table and accepted my offer of tea. "Who knows what the next person will be like."

I agreed with her; I hated it, but she was right. We were a tiny community. One bad resident would wreck the whole deal. "Did he own it?"

"No, dear." Delores sighed. "It's owned by a company and they rent it out. I hope they don't sell. You know how hard it is to keep our leases going. The marina is looking for any chance to get rid of us and rent to boats. They'd make more money that way."

There were some tricky legal steps to selling one of the houses. Not that long ago there were twenty homes down here, now we were only a handful. "I'm sure they'll continue to rent. It's valuable property."

I found an old cereal bowl, filled it with water and put it down for Mickey. Maybe I should go into Iain's one more time and get some food for him. I'd find Mickey a new owner, but not today. He didn't seem to mind the wound on his shoulder. Someone had put butterfly Band-Aids on it. I guess they worked as well as stitches for a small cut.

He slurped the water and looked up at me.

"I guess you want more," I said. The kettle boiled while I filled the bowl again. When the tea was steeping, I looked in the fridge and found a block of cheese. I cut it into chunks and put them on a plate. Mickey sniffed, and then knocked a couple onto the floor to eat them.

Delores and I stuck with tea and cookies. I didn't even try to get her to leave; she'd go when her goal was achieved. I just hoped that wasn't getting all kinds of confidential information from me.

She took a sip of her tea. "Have the police finished with us?"

"I don't know, Delores. I think they searched Iain's place, but that's no guarantee they won't come back." I dipped a cookie in my mug. Maybe I could get her to fill in some of the blanks. Delores would know about any secrets our neighbors held.

"Justin and I worry about you living all alone."

"Don't worry. Jake will be back soon enough. And I have a lot of security now." I pointed to the keypad beside the door.

"Iain had a woman there. Is she gone?"

I should probably start every case with a visit to Delores. I tried to hide my smile, but it was hard to resist feeling optimistic. "She's gone now." I saw her eyes narrow. "I have a key to check on the place until the owner decides what to do."

She didn't question the lie. "That's good to know. An empty house is like a beacon for thieves."

Mickey nudged my knee and then laid his head on my leg. I scratched his ears and that seemed to satisfy him.

Don't even think about trying to worm your way into staying with me.

"I love dogs," Delores said out of the blue. "Justin is allergic, so we can't have one. If you are keeping Mickey, I could take him for walks. And watch out for him."

Okay, that was kind Delores showing up. "I have to take him to the vet. I can't have a dog, anyway. I'm not reliable enough." And I wasn't giving her a key to my place.

"I noticed the cut. It doesn't look like it was done by a vet?" She did that all the time, end a statement like a question. I'm sure it worked with other people.

"I can't really talk about that."

Her tea was almost done. I'd only made half a pot so she wouldn't be getting a refill. Unless she had the USB, this was wasting my time. Maybe I could try her tactic. "He didn't have many visitors?" I said-asked.

"I noticed that too. I wonder if he had any family." She wasn't going to be fooled.

I gave up on the hints. "Did you know anything about him that would help the police?"

"Oh, I don't want the police at my door." Delores looked like I'd suggested she open a meth lab.

"I'll pass it along, don't worry." *Please let there be something.*

"There's nothing to pass along. The only person I saw him with was Mickey. Even that woman came and went by herself."

She drank the last of her tea and stood. "I'll talk to you later, Charity." She patted Mickey on her way to the door.

I may not have much new information, but I had Mickey, and that was a big step forward.

FORTY-NINE

I got another idea from Delores. It took almost a half hour to make the trip in my brain from hearing it, to processing, to realizing. Iain had only hung out with Mickey. Mickey had been taken by dognappers. Did Iain find a way to use his pet as a mule? It wouldn't hurt the dog if he did it right, but it was still creepy, or weird, or something not normal.

"Do you have a condom-wrapped USB in your belly?"

Mickey didn't answer the question. He looked at me, raising one eyebrow at a time, and gave a big sigh.

I wasn't conversant in dog.

Whether I was right or not, Mickey needed a vet to look at the cut on his shoulder. So, I called Dr. Lawson; he could take Mickey right away.

The dog probably needed a walk anyway. We stopped at Iain's place. Mickey was reluctant to go inside, but he did after I called him a couple of times. I attached a new collar and leash and picked up a bag of food. We delivered the food to my house and headed to the vet's.

"You found Mickey," a voice called.

I turned around to see a teenage boy with a French Bulldog trotting beside him on a black leash. "You know him?"

"Yeah. Angel and Mickey are friends. They dig holes together." He patted Mickey and the two dogs sniffed each other's butts in greeting. "I'm Gord."

I introduced myself. "Where does the excavation take place?" If Mickey had a friend, maybe Iain did too. And maybe the dogs were digging to find the USB.

"In the dog park." He pointed behind him. "Will you be there later?"

"Maybe, but Mickey has an appointment with the V.E.T. I might not make it today."

"How come you have Mickey? Is Iain away again?"

Gord seemed to know Iain better than even Delores. "Kind of. Did he go away often?"

"Once in a while. He'd go on some trip in his car. That is some kind of ride." Gord stopped speaking, the shine of car lust leaving his eyes as they narrowed. "What do you mean *did*?"

I passed on the information about Iain as gently as I could.

"Too bad. Are you Mickey's new family?" He patted the dog again.

"Just for a while. Do you know anyone who will take him?" The sooner I could find Mickey a new place to live the better.

"Maybe. I'll talk to my dad." He checked his phone. "Gotta go."

"Here's my card. If your dad says it's okay, give me a call."

He turned it over. "Private Investigator. Impressive."

I laughed. "Not as much as you imagine. Take care."

He tucked the card in his pocket and let his dog pull him toward the dog park.

I coaxed Mickey into a quick walk. We needed to be done with the vet as quickly as possible. I had a new place to search.

FIFTY

At Dr. Lawson's clinic, I sat patiently with Mickey, until a father and daughter came out of the back carrying a tortoise.

"See, Daddy, I knew he was going to be fine." She looked more relieved than confident.

Dr. Lawson waved me into the back room, gave Mickey a treat and started examining the wound. "Sorry about your human, Mickey."

"Is there anything else wrong with him?" The dog had been on his own for at least a day, there could be any number of parasites lurking in him waiting to come out all over my floor.

The doctor finished checking the cut then ran his hands all over Mickey.

"I'll clean the wound, but the dressing is fine, no point in disturbing it now." He grabbed some gauze and poured a clear liquid on it. I braced myself for the howl of pain. Dr. Larson laughed. "It won't hurt him."

He knew his stuff. Mickey tried to get away from the pad of gauze, but the vet held him gently. When he was satisfied, Dr. Lawson gave Mickey a second treat.

"He's probably hungry, and a little dehydrated. I didn't feel any ticks, so you shouldn't have to worry. He had a flea treatment not that long ago."

Good news for whoever took him in.

"How much trouble would it be to x-ray him?" I asked. "He may have something inside that would lead to Iain's killer."

"You mean something he swallowed?"

I nodded. "I'm looking for a USB, probably inside a condom or something."

He patted Mickey again. "So not an accident?"

"I don't think so. There's no guarantee it's in him, but if it is, he was fed it. Is that possible?"

"Yes. It would be like giving him a pill." He reached under Mickey and started feeling around. "How long do you think it's been there?"

"Maybe a day and a bit? I really don't know for sure." Poor Mickey just watched Dr. Lawson poke and prod him without complaining.

"Do you know when he was fed last?"

"I gave him some cheese an hour ago, but before that?" I shrugged. "He didn't seem super hungry."

Dr. Lawson stopped what he was doing, went to his desk, and checked something on his computer. "If it's urgent, I can schedule a scan in an hour. If you can wait, then we'll probably get it back in the morning."

I didn't think the killer would buy my story and wait until the morning. "It's urgent."

"You can leave Mickey with me tonight. I'll call you with the results." He tossed Mickey another treat. The dog caught it in midair and crunched it down.

"Will there be an image or something you can email me?" If it was there, I wasn't going to cut it out. An image would give me some bargaining power. Part of me hoped it was inside Mickey, and the other part didn't want it to be there. The dog didn't need to be in any more danger.

"I can do that." Dr. Lawson opened the door. "I'm guessing here, but you need to go, right? You are working on some kind of deadline?"

"Yeah. Take care of Mickey, okay?"

I had to find the mutt a new owner before I stupidly took him on.

I needed to talk to an adult human to get rid of this weird feeling of responsibility toward Iain's dog. Lu might still be packing for her trip with Matthieu; I'd never known her to be ready to go anywhere on a couple of hours' notice. A drive to West Vancouver and back would probably fill enough time to get the results of the scan. And an in-person visit would go a long way to repair whatever damage I'd done to our friendship. Iain's car wasn't going anywhere.

IT DIDN'T TAKE LONG to cross the bridge to West Vancouver. It was always iffy. In rush hour, you could count on it to take up to forty-five minutes, but rush hour had been over for at least a half hour. Any other time it was unpredictable; you could be looking at the back of a tour bus on the causeway for just as long as in peak traffic.

When I got to Lu's I parked in front because I would only be there a few minutes and knocked on the door. No one came, so I used my key, went inside, and turned off the alarm.

Lu's home was grand, that's the only word that fit. When she'd bought it with her first husband it had been about impressing the right people. When he'd died, she stayed because it was their home. I'm not sure what I would have done in the same circumstances, but it worked for Lu.

Normally the foyer was empty but for an antique table that

held a huge flower arrangement. Today there was a pair of shoes tossed at the bottom of the stairs and a scarf hanging on the newel post.

My heart started hammering.

I grabbed my phone and called Lu's cell. From the back of the house I heard it ringing. I ran toward the sound, terrified of what I'd find.

Had the killer actually meant that he'd start with my friends?

In the kitchen on the marble counter, Lu's phone happily rang in response to my call. Where would she go without her phone?

I called Matthieu while I rushed through the house. His phone went straight to voicemail. I left a message to call me.

Lu's bedroom was a mess; clothes tossed on the bed; jewelry scattered on the dresser. Her closet door was open, and more clothes were on the floor, shoes that would normally be in boxes were piled next to her outfits.

FIFTY-ONE

I called Leigh.

"Charity, do you have something for me?"

I blurted the words out in my hurry to get help. "Lu's place looks like it's been turned over."

"Does she think anything's been taken? Can I talk to her?" To her credit, Leigh sounded like it was a priority.

I'd forgotten the most important part. "She's not here. She said she was going away for a few days. I came to check her place, and found it trashed." As I spoke, I knew how weak it sounded.

"Okay. Was the door broken, or the lock busted?"

At least she wasn't telling me to calm down. "No. I used my key when I got here." Then it dawned on me that the alarm was on when I came in. I felt like a fool, and all I could use to explain my freak out was the pretty absent threat from the guy in the parking lot. I needed to get off the phone as quickly as possible without tripping Leigh's suspicious nature.

"Can you tell if anything is gone?" she asked, forestalling my goodbye.

I looked around and realized that if this was a robbery, there wouldn't be about ten thousand dollars' worth of jewels laying on the dresser. And the TV downstairs would have been taken. "I don't think so. Yeah, I know. She's an adult. She said she would be away. There's no reason to think it's anything other than a rush to get packed."

Leigh didn't speak for a moment.

"It's fine," I said. "Go back to the murders. I don't have anything real on those either."

I hadn't meant it to sound so bitter. I knew how the cops had to prioritize, and I knew I had reason to be paranoid. Unfortunately, I also knew that Lu, and Val for that matter, would disappear on me sometimes for no reason.

"Charity, if it was anyone else, I'd agree. But you know Lu, is this how she'd leave her house? Has anyone made threats?"

She was trying and it did help reduce my panic. "Maybe if they were in a big hurry to leave. I guess she'd give the housekeeper a bonus for tidying up. And, no, I haven't had any threats against my friends." I left out the threat against me until I needed it to motivate the cops to come tonight.

"I'll see if the West Van police have any reason to worry, but let's wait a while. If Lu and Matthieu had to get a flight, maybe they'll call and set your mind at ease."

The panic was almost gone. Leigh was right. If they decided at the last minute where they were going, they wouldn't have time to clean up the mess. I took the opportunity to get some information on the Mickey case as I was beginning to think of it. "Are you making any progress?"

"We're waiting for results on fingerprints. There were a lot. I think the place was party central for anyone in the neighborhood. We're doing a door-to-door, but we haven't found anything yet."

"Make sure they talk to Mr. Ozwald. He keeps an eye on

the neighborhood." The words came out before I engaged my thinking filter.

"How do you know that?"

Damn, damn, damn. "I had to talk to the neighbors before I went in. Sorry I guess I forgot to mention it." Would she let me off the hook?

"And by I, you mean you and Val?"

"Someone already told you."

"Is there anything else you're holding back?"

"Will you talk to Val? She didn't see anything, or touch anything. You know how she'll be if you bring her in."

Leigh sighed. "I'll recommend we talk to her later, and only if we can't find any other leads. Don't think I didn't notice you dodged my question."

"Fine. I'm not holding back anything you could use for the case, or for your career. Anything I have is too... vague right now. I promise you'll hear from me as soon as there's enough for you to follow up on. I promise that it will be you, and not anyone else." This time I held back the annoyance from my voice. Leigh was trying to do her job.

"Call my personal number, Charity. I'm off shift soon."

I said I would, and we ended the call on civil terms. I took that as a sign of me becoming more mature. Val's phone went straight to voicemail, not unusual enough to worry me. Or, maybe, my panic at Lu's had burned me out. I left her a message that the cops might come knocking and to be civil, and maybe get Rory's dad to help. With Rance in the room, Val would have a harder time pissing the cops off just for fun.

FIFTY-TWO

I was home by the time Dr. Lawson called. When I saw the name on the caller ID, I got dizzy with hope. Not that I'm usually that emotional, and maybe I needed food, and maybe it was just the frustration, but maybe it was hope.

"I'm sorry, Charity," he said.

"No contraband?" There was no other way to interpret his tone.

"The good news is that Mickey wasn't permanently hurt. He needs a rest, and a bit of stability, then he'll be just like new."

"Thanks, how much do I owe you?" I crossed my fingers; animal care could be costly, and I wasn't going to get any more money from this case.

"I'll charge Iain's estate," he said. "It wasn't that much, but whoever inherits will get Mickey too."

I didn't like to think of the dog as being like a vase or an investment portfolio. "What do you think would happen if I found Mickey new owners?"

"I'm not a lawyer, but I've seen this a few times in my practice. Find out what the estate lawyer thinks. If the heir isn't a dog person, they'll probably be happy for you to take care of it."

"Shall I come pick him up?" I'd start working on Mickey's new family as soon as I was done with this USB situation.

"Let him stay here until tomorrow," Dr. Lawson said. "You can come and get him in the morning. Maybe take him for his walk?"

He was trying to matchmake.

"I'm not the right kind of girl for a dog relationship. I'm unreliable and inconsistent." He laughed. "I'll come by in the morning. Maybe I'll know what the will says by then."

That was the end of that lead.

My next call was to Leigh. Maybe she would know who was handling the will. It might be too soon, but if I told her it was for Mickey's sake, maybe she'd tell me the name of the lawyer. Then, fingers crossed the lawyer would have an envelope that was to be opened in the event of Iain's suspicious death. One that held a USB and an explanation.

She picked up right away. "Do you have anything?"

As if I was the one who'd get information first. Well, fair enough, it was probably why I was an asset to her.

"Nothing concrete, yet. I may have something for you in a couple of hours," I said.

"Then why call?"

I heard voices in the background. Leigh was somewhere crowded. "Am I interrupting something?"

The noise faded. I guess she was getting somewhere quiet. "Just a family thing. I have to get back to it."

"Fine, I'll be quick. Do you know what's happening with Iain's estate?"

There was a pause and I wondered if I'd overstepped or just been too rude and pushy.

She finally asked, "How will that solve the murder?"

I hated to disappoint her. "It won't, but I have his dog. I need to know if I should be giving Mickey to someone. It's hard to find clues on the case, if I have to keep running back to take care of the dog." She didn't need to know it wasn't true. If Leigh had enough confidence in me, she'd want me on the case, not scooping poop.

"Okay. Fine," she said. "I don't have it yet, but I know the detectives were doing a search for family members, wills, and anything that would connect us to someone who knew him. If the will is registered, we'll know the lawyer by morning."

Too late if the mythical envelope existed. It wouldn't help to tell Leigh that, or anything else until I needed her help. "I'll hang on to Mickey until we know."

I promised again that I'd call with anything I found before ending the call.

FIFTY-THREE

I felt like I was spinning in a circle. If I couldn't locate the USB in the next hour or two, I would have to come up with a plan B. My current Plan A was to walk away from the encounter, rather than ride in an ambulance, with or without lights and sirens. I couldn't implement that without the actual USB or some facsimile.

My list of places to look had dwindled to a very few. I could go back to the house where Iain was killed, maybe he'd taken it with him. The dog park. If Mickey and his buddy dug holes there, would Iain have used one to hide the flash-drive?

I suppose I could also call Leigh again. Maybe the cops had found it and bagged it as evidence. But if I was going to search the house, I'd have to do that before reaching out to Leigh because three calls in succession with no help might piss her off. I grabbed my car keys and remembered that I hadn't checked Iain's car. The panic about Lu had driven Gord's words out of my head. I knew he drove a red Audi Roadster. And it hadn't been parked outside the crime scene. We all rented spaces from the hotel car park, so I'd find his there — I hoped.

On the way, I took another look at the off-leash park. It was definitely not a place where I would keep anything. The ground was torn up by dogs running around, holes looked like they were excavated daily. Another possibility crossed off the list. I wandered the parking lot until I found Iain's car. It wasn't the kind of vehicle that you could open with something most women kept in their purses. Then again, I wasn't like most women. I pulled out my Slim Jim and slid it down the window. It took a couple of tries, but there was no one around so I could take my time. The alarm was easy to deal with, and before it did more than chirp a few times, I was sitting in the driver's seat patting down the upholstery.

People who paid this much for a car probably didn't realize how easy it was to break into with a little practice. I had Matthieu to thank for my breaking and entering skills.

The USB was nowhere in the upholstery, under the floor mats, in the glove box, or any other place I could look without destroying the car. I popped the hood and the trunk. Checking the engine was a long shot, the heat would probably destroy electronic devices that weren't supposed to be there. But I took a look anyway; nothing that didn't look like it belonged.

The trunk was empty.

I didn't think Mickey spent any time in the car. It was pristine, as if it had just come off the lot. Or been cleaned to cover up evidence.

I closed everything and locked the door. The cops would find it soon enough; I wasn't going to waste time calling anyone about the location of a worthless lead.

I called the number Sara had given me earlier, but the phone was out of service. I debated calling her husband, but if she hadn't gone home, then that would be cruel and, more importantly, useless.

Now without a place to search, I was out of options. I'd have to fake something for the hand-off. It probably wouldn't matter to the cops, but if the killer got away, he'd come for revenge. Of that I was sure.

FIFTY-FOUR

I could buy a fake USB on my way to the meet so I could rest for an hour. I'd been running around the best part of two days, and I needed a nap. I also needed food and something to take my mind off tonight. There was always the possibility that concentrating on something else would bring up an idea from the deep recesses.

My cooking skills were basic, and I preferred to defrost and heat rather than create from scratch. I'd had too many meals go horribly wrong to bother trying to improve. I opened my freezer and grabbed a frozen entree and saw what I'd dropped there yesterday: the bag with a piece of Mickey and his collar.

The Mickey bit was frozen solid, and I knew it didn't contain the USB because I'd done a thorough squish looking for his locator chip. And the hunk of flesh wasn't big enough. And I didn't think Iain had been in possession of the thing long enough to embed it in his dog.

The collar was another thing altogether. It was about an inch wide, black leather, metal studs piercing the length of it. Not round ones with spikes, like you might see on a bulldog or pit bull, but kind of lozenge shaped, and they were different sizes. The ones near the end, where the buckle would close were about a half inch, then they got bigger to the center one, which was more than an inch by my estimate.

I felt along the edges of the large stud. It was tight to the leather. I could cut it off, but Iain had probably made it so he could get at the USB without destroying the collar. I checked the back, but it was just leather, the studs were covered with a separate thin, smooth layer; I guess to protect the dog's neck. When I inspected the edge, I saw the line where the two layers were glued together. And at the center of the collar, the seal was more visible.

I reached for a paring knife then wiggled it between the badly glued leather. It gave way like it was Post-it note glue. Inside, tucked into the hollow back of the center stud was a USB wrapped in cling film. I could just make out the scarab on the case.

Relief blew through me like a summer breeze. I had it. Now I just needed to know what it was. Okay, maybe I didn't need to know, but I really wanted to know. What could be on this little drive that was worth killing three people for?

I opened my laptop and plugged the drive in. When I clicked on it, a password window opened. I guess it was too much to hope that something this important would be easy to access. It was probably highly encrypted, but no one would be able to tell that I'd tried. I ran a password cracking app and sat back.

A half hour later, the program was still running, and I had eaten a frozen dinner. Nothing from the computer, but my brain had stewed over a plan. I wasn't going to just hand over something this important. If the killer got away, he'd have what he wanted, and maybe he'd tie up some loose ends. Like me and Val.

At least Lu hadn't been anywhere near the case.

I'd take a substitute along with me and try to get away with that. I'd have the real one, just in case. I still had some time to let the program run, but I needed to go shopping and there was no way I'd leave that behind. I canceled the password cracker, ejected the USB, and tucked it into a secure pocket in my bag.

Before I left, I called Val. Her voicemail answered right away meaning her phone was off. "Listen, the killer may have seen you at the house. Maybe stick with Rory for the rest of the day."

It wasn't the way I intended to warn her, but at least she had a message. I'd take the backlash if there was any.

FIFTY-FIVE

As I stopped to lock my door, I saw our local Realtor striding down the finger dock. She specialized in the sale and rental of floating homes. Our market might be tiny, but in the whole Lower Mainland, there were about thirty communities, and it made a nice living for a few agents. Ilene kept in contact with us about three times a year just so we wouldn't go anywhere else if we decided to move. She dressed for downtown, conservative heels, knee-length skirt, blouse, and jacket. Her blond hair pulled back in a chic bun.

"Charity, how are you doing?" She cornered me, in a nice 'I'm being friendly' way.

"Great. You know how it is living down here. Nothing is ever as bad as it could be." I slid my keys into my pocket to indicate I was going, not coming, so I wasn't going to ask her in for coffee. "You're here about Iain's place." It couldn't be anything else. There was only Jake's and Iain's home after mine.

She hesitated. I guess it might be confidential, or she wasn't sure how much the police would let her share. "Yeah. I need to make a report to the owner and then we'll be renting it out again."

"I was in there," I admitted. I wasn't going to give the key back unless she asked. They'd change the locks for a new tenant anyway. "It's a bit of a mess. Who will be cleaning it up? Do you know?"

"The police came by the office. I gave them his rental agreement. There's a sister somewhere in the States. They'll call her. I guess she'll give us instructions."

It was a relief that someone would miss him. Even a thief and a cheater like Iain should make a difference in the world when they die. "What about the dog?"

She frowned. "What dog? His lease specified no pets."

I guess his damage deposit was forfeit. "He had a black lab. I didn't see any pet damage when I was there."

Ilene rolled her eyes. "That's lucky, but we'll have to get it specially cleaned. If someone has allergies, the fact that a dog lived there will be a deterrent to leasing it. Where's the animal now?"

She assumed I would know. That was interesting. Did she think we all knew everything there was to know about our neighbors? I couldn't rouse any feeling of resentment at her assumption because — well, I did know. "He's with the vet. I'll get someone to find out if the sister wants him. If not, we'll find another home. I promise he won't spend any more time in the house. If you find dog stuff, like food, you can drop it off at my door."

"Thanks, Charity. So, are you still happy living down here? I could get you a great price. People are looking at floating homes as an affordable alternative."

I laughed. "Where would I go? I own in downtown Vancouver. I can't afford anything else. I can't move out to the suburbs either." It would be good to have a new neighbor, too.

She glanced toward Iain's home. "People change their mind. Just call me if you do, okay?"

I promised and then said goodbye. There was a USB waiting to be bought.

FIFTY-SIX

When I got back home, there was a bag of dog treats, two collars, and a container of poop sacks waiting on my doorstep. I was ready to provide foster care for Mickey if I needed to.

The trip had been fruitful. I had two USBs that looked close to the actual one. The cases were the same color, they were the same size, but there was no scarab. What I did have was a plastic etching gun and a pot of blue paint that matched. All I needed to do was carefully etch the scarab then paint it. Hence two USBs. I figured the chances were high that my first attempt would go horribly wrong.

The walk had given me some time to think as well. I had to take control of the meeting. I wasn't going to wait for this guy at a deserted house. I was going to change the location but keep the time. I wanted somewhere public enough so I would be safe, and not too crowded. I wasn't going to be responsible for an innocent bystander getting hurt.

And I needed time to get Leigh and her detectives in place. I propped Mickey's things in the corner beside the couch and then made the call.

The killer didn't pick up. This was a problem because there

was no voicemail prompt. If I couldn't get to him, I couldn't make the changes. If I couldn't do that, I wasn't in control.

Putting the phone down, I laid out the etching tools on the kitchen counter. Whatever happened next, I could, at least, be ready with the decoy. The paint was supposed to dry hard in about ten minutes. Plenty of leeway.

I plugged in the etching gun and placed the real USB scarab side up, and then unwrapped the two victims. The real scarab was also etched. I ran my finger along the design and could feel the slight markings under the enamel. Who enamels a freaking USB?

The light on the side of the gun turned green. It was ready.

My phone rang.

It was the same number I'd called. So, he was screening me.

"Why did you call?" He was short on phone etiquette.

"We need to meet somewhere else. I'm not going back to that street. I want a more public place." As I said it out loud, I realized how stupid I would be to go to a dark empty street. I should have negotiated this right up front.

"I set the rules."

"You want your data. You accept my change." I grabbed a side plate from the cupboard and slipped the gun onto it. The last thing I needed was a burn mark on my counter to remind me of this case forever.

He didn't speak, and I couldn't hear any background noise. Nothing to indicate that the call was coming from the airport, or a convenient train whistle from a close by track, or anything else that could help me find him. Not like a movie at all. But it wasn't just him thinking. I'd been put on hold, or maybe he'd covered the microphone. If he had a partner, I was screwed.

"I have a hostage."

My heart stopped. Every job that got dangerous seemed to include kidnapping me or one of my friends. "Who is it?"

"You don't need to know. If you want to change the location, the hostage will pay for it."

I took a deep breath. This was the point where I took control or I lost it completely. If he had a hostage, and I wasn't quite sure I believed him, then they were valuable. He wouldn't do anything drastic to lose the edge. At least that's what I told myself.

"I'm not coming to that street. You'll kill me and the hostage. No one will know." I hoped my voice came across as confident, because I felt sick and ready to pass out.

"Do you have what I asked for?"

If he was still talking, I had some leverage. "Not with me." I didn't want him barging into my house. "I found it. I hid it in a safe place. I'll bring it with me to Robson Square at the time we agreed."

"You'll bring it to the original location."

"I changed the deal. You don't agree, then you don't get the data. I'll hand it over to the police." I held my breath and felt my heart pound in my ears.

"If you do that, I'll kill my hostage."

I don't believe him. I don't believe him. I kept repeating it in my mind as I said, "That's four murders at least." Then I hit end call.

As soon as I did, my knees gave out and I was crouched on the floor shaking. Had I just killed someone I loved?

FIFTY-SEVEN

I was sure it took an hour or more to get control of my body. When I checked the phone, it was only two minutes. My hands were still a bit shaky, so I took a bunch of deep breaths to get rid of the adrenalin in my system. Then I altered the USBs. I guess the fight or flight reaction gives you great focus, because the first fake was as perfect as I needed. I left it drying on the counter and started packing my bag with anything that might help me save myself and whoever the hostage was.

The only thing I could do was go to the original location at the agreed time. I wanted to be ready to head out as soon as I called Leigh so she wouldn't have a chance to stop me. And I was going to be there early enough to find every escape route that existed.

I picked up my phone to get Leigh involved and it rang.

The killer.

Panic started to steal my breath again, but I answered the call.

"Changed your mind?" Keeping my voice steady took all of my energy, but I had to pretend that I was in control of myself and of the situation.

"We'll meet at Robson square. I'm not going to wait. You be there in a half hour." He was gone.

Okay. Positive side, I wasn't going to have to wait around, and the decoy was ready. Negative side, I had no chance to scope out the area. Although I knew it well, I hadn't looked at it in this light before. Mental note to always look for escape routes. Bigger negative. Would Leigh be ready in time?

The decoy was dry so that went into my pocket, the real one into my bag. It was only ten minutes to walk to Robson Square. It might feel like I was on a deadline, but I had breathing time.

I called Leigh.

"You have something this time?" she asked brusquely.

"Yes." I gave her the details. "Can you get people there?"

"Charity, promise me next time you'll give us more warning?"

I tried for a laugh, but it was more of a grunt. "There isn't going to be a next time."

She did manage a laugh. "Oh, don't kid yourself. This stuff seems to find you attractive."

That was hard to argue with. "Will you be there?"

"Yes. And thanks for calling me."

It would give her the boost she needed to get into the homicide department.

"One more thing," I said.

"There always is."

"You guys have Iain's will yet? You know how to contact his sister?"

"Yes."

"Can you ask her about Mickey? The dog."

"Is this urgent?"

I wanted to say yes, but really it wouldn't make a difference to what happened next. "No, but I don't want him to go to a shelter. He's at the vet, Dr. Lawson's practice. If she doesn't want him, we'll find him a home."

"You could have asked me this later."

"In case something goes wrong." I sounded pathetic in my own ears.

"It won't. But, yes, I'll find out for you."

I swallowed a crying jag. I had to get going. "How will I know you are there?"

"Charity, don't worry. We'll see *you*. Don't look for us or the guy will know. Just be careful. We can't get the civilians out of there without raising suspicion."

Was I no longer a civilian? Sadly, that made me feel better. "I need to go."

"Don't do anything until the agreed time. We need to get in place."

I promised.

FIFTY-EIGHT

Robson Square is outside the Vancouver Art Gallery and a place where protests happen and tourists walk through. The steps to the art gallery are a mini version of the Spanish Steps in Rome some days; people sitting on the stairs talking, eating lunch, reading. Food carts cluttered the sidewalks and gave off aromas of hotdogs and onions grilling. Not far away designer stores displayed their stylish items. It didn't seem a dangerous place. Then again, Fellini made a career out of this kind of scene turning into something bizarre in a second.

It was a little quieter than usual, maybe just a lull between before and after dinner strolls. Traffic crawled between red lights and pigeons strutted in mobs in the forecourt.

There was no sign of my hoodie-wearing killer. Although there were four men who had the same build. I wondered how he would make contact.

Five minutes of casually watching, and I couldn't tell who were the cops and who were the civilians. It was impossible not to try to figure out if I had coverage, despite agreeing with Leigh that the killer would probably notice my change of attitude.

Right now, I felt alone and on a ledge fifty floors above the street even though my feet were firmly planted on the ground.

Waiting let my mind stew over whether the hostage was real. And if so, was it Lu, or Val? I couldn't imagine Matthieu being taken. And the fact that he hadn't called was evidence that Lu was safe — unless he was unconscious, or dead.

If not my friends, was there someone else that I'd care enough about to let a killer go? Not Jake, he was safe thirteen thousand kilometers away. I had my call to look forward to. That was a bright spark in this grim situation.

I couldn't sit still any longer. The Square also went below ground where there is an open ice rink and UBC had a campus. Now that I thought of it, downstairs was a much more likely handover place. Still open, but less populated.

I strolled casually over to the bank of stairs leading down, no one followed me, no one even seemed interested. Maybe the cops weren't there yet. Maybe I was on my own. That thought didn't make me any less jumpy.

I went down to the bottom level and pretended to look around for something. It felt a bit like I was doing an acting exercise. The one where you practice reactions to experiences.

I'm not good at pretending to be anything except confident, so I looked for a washroom. All that did is make me need to pee. I put it out of my mind and concentrated on trying to see if anyone seemed to be looking at me.

There were a few people around; mostly students and tourists. Still no one who would pass for the killer. And definitely no one who had a hostage. I wondered if he'd changed his mind.

I checked my phone; it was ten minutes past the time he'd given me. If he was playing a game to get me back to the first location, I was screwed. I couldn't just say no because I didn't know if he was lying about the hostage.

And he knew where I lived.

And he was willing to kill.

There wasn't much to look at in the window, just the entrance to UBC. I couldn't reasonably hang out here much longer. And I did need a washroom. The campus was still open and would be for almost an hour. There was bound to be a public washroom in the lobby.

I headed for the sign with the woman in the A-line dress. The actual facilities were down a hall and around the corner. I would be safe here.

As I passed a service door, it swung open. Someone grabbed my arm and dragged me inside.

FIFTY-NINE

I held out my free hand to stop my headlong rush into the wall. The space behind the door was the landing to a stairwell. I was hoping it would lead to a very public, and cop filled, street.

Turning I pulled my arm out of his grasp and looked into the blue eyes of the man who killed Iain and who knows how many other people. I tried to commit him to memory in case I survived and he got away. A head taller than me, slim build, dark-brown hair brushed back from his forehead. I pegged his age at late thirties, not quite getting that lived-in look of the forties, but not fresh and young either. No visible scars or tattoos. I'd be able to pick him out of a line-up, but I'm not sure I could give the cops enough to get him into one.

"You're late," I said before I could stop myself. Not the time to irritate the guy. And not the place. We were alone. If any of the people in the square or on the other side of the door were cops, they couldn't see what was going on.

"I needed to make sure you were alone." His words were measured. He was holding back on more than anger.

He moved toward me.

I backed up one step.

"What now?"

"Hand over the USB."

I smiled. Once he had the freaking data he'd kill me, and no one would know he'd been here. The smile was for him. For me, I wanted to scream. Loud and long enough for someone to stop him.

"You have it with you?" He took another step forward.

"I'm not stupid." My voice shook a little, betraying the lie of my bravado. I ignored it. "I'll tell you how to get it when I know I'm safe." That would have been a great idea if only I'd thought of it an hour ago.

"I don't think so." He took a step up, forcing me against the wall. "I could just kill you first, and then search you."

True.

"And when you don't find it? I get the idea you have a deadline. How is starting over going to help you with that?"

He leaned closer. I got a scent of lemon and sage from him. I'd be able to identify his aftershave. He had that polished look of money, maybe it was a signature scent.

It was getting hard to breathe through the panic. I couldn't keep quiet though. There was always the chance that the cops would stumble on us. Leigh knew me well enough that she wouldn't have to strain her imagination too much to think I'd stranded myself out of sight of help because I was impatient.

I wasn't going to make my call with Jake. I felt my heart squeeze at the thought someone would call him with the news of my death.

This guy was going to kill me. I had no doubt about that. There was something in his eyes, his tone that said he had no fear of me.

"You wouldn't have agreed to the meeting if you didn't have it."

He ran his hand down my left arm to my hip, then felt for my back pockets. I wanted to throw up.

"What about your hostage?"

"What about her?"

So, it was a woman. That didn't help me identify who I was putting in danger. "I want her safe before I hand it over."

He stepped back, apparently bored with feeling me up. I hoped it wasn't because he'd decided I'd be easier to search dead.

"I'll let her go when I have my USB." Now his voice was less confident.

I kept pushing. "No. I need to see who it is, and that she's alive, and then you'll let her go. I won't have someone else die."

"My, aren't you the brave one?" He glanced around. I don't know what caught his attention, but no one burst through the door to save me.

"Are you going to do it? Show me your hostage?"

He shrugged. "Might as well." He pulled a phone out of his pocket and tapped the screen. "Here."

SIXTY

Sara Lyman.

The screen showed her sitting on a chair. Her hands tied behind her back, her feet held together with duct tape, and her mouth covered with another strip of tape.

I looked from the phone to his face. It was cold and calm. "How do I know you haven't killed her?"

"Look at the time stamp." He pushed the phone closer to me.

It was in the corner of the screen. It showed that the photo was taken fifteen minutes ago.

"You could have killed her right after you took the picture. If that stamp is even real." If I could keep him talking, maybe someone would come: a cop, a tourist. Anyone. I didn't let myself wonder why someone would open a service door. Or remember that the campus would be closing soon.

"It's not like I can call her up and let you chat." He laughed. "She's all tied up."

He thought he was in control. I wasn't going to let him get his hands on even the fake USB without knowing Sara was free. She didn't deserve to be in that position. She fell for Iain and lost him to murder. Her marriage was probably ruined, and now she was in the hands of someone who was quite capable of killing to get his way. I had the creepy feeling that he was starting to enjoy the murder part of his day.

"Who are you?" I just needed his attention taken away for a second. If I could get a few inches of space, I'd run to the top of the stairs; there must be an exit door there. He might catch me, but at least I'd be out and in view of anyone on the street. "I think I know you."

"Do you really expect me to tell you my identity? To detail my evil plan so you have time to work out a way to stop me?"

"It was worth a try." I shifted my weight to the side as I shrugged. "I just think I've seen your face recently. But not in these clothes. You were in a suit."

Then I remembered. It was the eyes. I must have forgotten to put on my poker face. He leaned back in surprise, giving me some space. I just needed a little more room to be able to run.

"Who do you think I am?"

"Devon Bergeron. You're the head of DeBerg Corp. Is the data something to do with that?" I tried to make the words accusatory, but they just sounded frightened.

I'd surprised him. He started to smile and then got control again. "Good guess. Why don't you try telling me what's on the USB?"

That was a trick. He wanted me to look, or touch, or somehow give away the location of the USB. I was smarter than that — not much, after all I was here alone with a murderer.

"You do investments, right?" It was a wild guess.

"No. Data security." He was entering CEO mode, and as he spoke, he took one step back.

I had just enough room to get past him. I took it.

One step up toward the exit that had to be there.

He reached for me.

I pulled away and took another step.

I yelled, but it didn't sound very loud panic tightening my lungs and turning down the volume on my vocal cords. Even if a student was walking through the lobby, they wouldn't hear it.

He followed me up, reaching for my arm.

I realized that my plan was stupid but tried for a burst of speed anyway. There were only about twenty steps to the top, but that was a long, long way.

He managed to grab my arm and pull. I felt something tear and then the pain flooded me. I slid down the walls to sit on the step.

"No more stupid moves," he whispered right next to my ear. Then he stepped back and looked me over.

The agony was ebbing, so maybe not a broken bone. I wiggled my fingers; they worked. I glanced at my arm. It wasn't twisted in the wrong direction. I would heal. And if I could handle the pain, I could use the arm.

"Why did you do that?" He seemed genuinely puzzled. It was like he'd never faced opposition in his life. "I told you I would find it easier to check a dead body. You know I am capable of killing."

"Why haven't you killed me yet?" If he'd killed Iain and the two dognappers, he wouldn't hesitate to do the same to me. "Lost your taste for it?"

I saw the change in him as he tried to get his emotions under control. His face relaxed, his breathing slowed. I'd hit something that shocked him back to sanity — or, at least, from the edge of murder.

"It would be hard to explain searching a corpse if someone came by." He relaxed completely, leaning against the railing.

In my mind, I saw me rushing to push him over the railing and down to the hard concrete below. It wasn't far, but maybe it would do some damage.

In real life, my arm still throbbed so much it made me feel sick even thinking about moving. And the railing was annoyingly up to code and too high for me to succeed.

"Are we going to be here all night?" I asked.

Leigh might come looking eventually, but I knew he was on some kind of deadline. If I could get him talking again, maybe I could find out what that was.

"No. Give me the USB."

My plan with the fake USB was feeling stupider now that I might have to use it. There was too much light here for it to pass. If I handed it over, would that be my last action?

"I don't get it. Why are you so patient?" I was starting to doubt my deadline theory.

He glanced down as the door clicked and then opened.

SIXTY-ONE

My heart slowed from hummingbird levels. This was going to be a cop.

It wasn't.

Sara stepped through and closed it behind her. A big smile on her face, but she wasn't looking at me. She was staring at Bergeron.

Mental tumblers started falling into place. If Sara wasn't a hostage, and she was in on it, then Iain wasn't her steppingstone.

"You weren't with Iain at all," I said. "Did you break in? Did I interrupt your search?"

"Smart. Well, it's too late for it, but congratulations, anyway." She moved to stand beside Bergeron, cutting off my hopes to escape down the stairs.

My instincts were so far off, I wondered if I was in the wrong line of business. "So, what's on the USB that's worth three lives?"

Her hand slipped into the pocket of her coat, bringing out a gun. "Three you know of."

A quiver started in my gut. I knew that feeling. The beginning of an adrenalin flood. Could I use it? "Why?"

"Devon and I have plans. That USB is the key to getting us rich enough to be outside the law."

So, she was willing to talk. Just my luck that she was also the one with the gun. "You killed them, right? Three bodies in that house. You came here with the gun. Devon can't bring himself to do what it takes."

She laughed and used the gun to gesture for me to stand. I managed a half-crouch. "Now I understand why all the killers on TV blab at the end. It's oddly arousing to tell you the truth when I know you'll never be able to pass it on."

Devon kept his eyes on me. He wasn't a brainwashed tool. This plan was just as much his work as Sara's. She might do the killing, but he liked to watch.

"So, blab," I said.

"Sure. The USB has code on it that unlocks some nice juicy databases. We'll prove to the people who care about the information that they are vulnerable, and then we'll get paid. And they'll pay big."

The pain was down to a dull throb, maybe the adrenalin was responsible. Whatever the reason, my mind had room for escape plans again. If she shot me here, the noise would bring people and they'd have no time to search me. If I couldn't escape from this location, I could probably do it when they moved me.

"Wouldn't someone say no? Or, wouldn't some of these victims have resources to find you?" I didn't know enough about an organization that might have information worth enough money, but if they did, there was a Sara and Devon on the payroll.

"They won't have time to look for us." She put her hand in the other pocket and drew out a cylinder that she screwed on to the end of the gun.

Great. Now they could kill me without making a lot of noise.

"I told him that I wasn't stupid enough to bring the thing with me." I just had to keep them talking. Time was my only tool.

"And I don't believe that either. You thought you were rescuing someone — me. You wouldn't have taken the risk."

Devon was looking a lot paler than before. The idea of watching Sara kill me might be getting to him. Or, maybe he realized that he could be taking the second bullet.

"Maybe there's another option?" I looked at Devon as I spoke. If he was squeamish, I figured I could get him to help.

Sara shook her head. "If you don't want to watch, babe, go. You can keep people away from the door."

"We could buy her silence," he said, not taking her up on the offer.

Sara rolled her eyes, but she turned her attention back to me. "How much to hand it over and go on your way?"

"Ten million." I lied.

"See," Sara said giving Devon a nudge. "She's not a good liar. We might be able to buy the USB, but she'd never keep quiet."

"No. I would." I lied again, but she wasn't fooled.

"You've got until I count to three."

What happened to a count of ten?

"Fine." I reached over with my good arm and pulled the homemade USB from my pocket. "Here. Now can I go?"

She snatched the drive from my hand. It was unsettling the way her face changed. She started out looking like a stone-cold killer, eyes narrow, lips thinned, no emotion showing at all, then shifted to greed and that glee pulled a smile on her lips.

And now to rage. As soon as she touched the USB her face flushed, and she raised the gun.

"This is a fake."

Devon took the USB from her and rubbed his thumb along

the scarab. Even from my terrified crouch, I could see the blue rub off. So, dry didn't actually mean the same thing to the manufacturer of the paint as it did to the rest of us.

The gun was pointing at me. No tremor in Sara's grip.

"If you kill me, you won't find it." The hidden pocket in my bag wasn't exactly foolproof, but they were in a hurry. I hoped they would miss it. If I was going to die, I wanted to know they wouldn't win.

"Devon, search her."

"Don't shoot me by mistake," he said, with a little laugh.

"I'll try my best."

Why did I get the feeling that she was going to do the opposite? If Sara had the technical skills, and the connections to use the data, she didn't need Devon. From what I'd seen, he wouldn't go easily. They were still working together because they needed each other. If I had to guess, Devon was planning to get rid of Sara as soon as he didn't need a killer. It wouldn't be by his hand; he'd hire someone for sure.

Sara kept the gun on me. "Take the bag first."

Devon yanked the bag off my shoulder, and pushed me away, banging my head against the wall. The pain woke my arm's receptors and the initial agony flashed and then subsided. I struggled to hang onto my thinking ability.

He emptied the contents on the stairs, and my belongings rolled down bouncing off the corner and continuing down to the refuge area. He glanced to make sure there was no scarab-decorated USB in the cascade and then started squeezing the sides and bottom of the bag. It took seconds.

"There's something in the bottom." He pulled a multitool out of his pocket. "I never thought I'd get to use this," he said to Sara holding it up.

"It's a new adventure every day with me." She grinned again. "Not too long now, Charity."

Things went gray as my body focused on keeping my vital organs working. Unfortunately, neither flight nor fight were an option. I was trapped, injured, and out of time.

Devon slashed at the bottom of my bag, then dug out his property. "Shoot her."

Sara checked that he had the USB and then turned to me. "Not so fast. I think she needs to know how much she's pissed me off. I'll kill her when she's sorry."

She handed the gun to Devon, and said, "Don't shoot me."

I tried to get up. I couldn't get my legs to work properly.

I had a plan. If I ran, maybe I'd just get wounded. But I couldn't lever myself out of the crouch.

Sara stepped in close and poked my injured arm. I screamed.

She laughed and punched my shoulder.

I screamed through the pain. The world was getting darker as my body tried to go unconscious to avoid hurting.

I heard a bang in the distance, but no additional pain.

"Freeze!" It was a man. It was loud and it was commanding.

I saw Devon drop the gun. Sara grabbed it and pointed it at the newcomer. Then I heard a really loud bang.

Sara folded up and collapsed. Devon tried to move backward but someone was there; all I could see was a blur of dark blue.

Then I passed out.

SIXTY-TWO

I woke up on a gurney in the back of the ambulance. There was a paramedic clipping an oxygen tube to my nose.

"Welcome back," she said. Then, turning to someone at the back door, she added, "She's awake."

Leigh moved into my line of sight. "Can you get a case that doesn't end with you in an ambulance?"

I grinned. They must have given me something for the pain because nothing hurt. "What took you so long?"

She rolled her eyes. "You went down to the lower level. Then you disappeared. Good thing there's only one place you could be. Just a few more doors to look through than I expected."

"I was in there for a long time." I tried not to whine, but I wasn't successful.

"You were in there maybe five minutes. Next time you ask for a police presence, follow the rules, okay?"

I nodded. It was hard to bring up any kind of emotion through the numbness. "You got them both, right?"

"Yes." Leigh looked over her shoulder. "Look, I shouldn't say this, but you did me a big favor by feeding me this information. We listened at the door to that last bit. We heard every-thing and got most of it on record."

"You let me get beat up?" I tried to sit and realized my arm was immobilized.

"Nasty strain and some torn ligaments," the paramedic said. "They'll confirm it at the hospital. We need to get going."

"Just a second." Leigh leaned in close.

I was pretty sure the paramedic would hear what was said. Then Leigh asked her to give us some privacy.

"If anyone asks, make sure you explain exactly how it went down."

I wasn't likely to lie. I guess Leigh knew I'd keep something back if I could. "Any details in particular?"

She glanced to make sure we were alone. "That you knew exactly the risks. I know we didn't discuss it, Charity, but I don't want these two getting off because they find a hole in the proce-dure. You knew we'd be recording, right?"

The drugs were probably messing up my reasoning. Was Leigh asking me to make something up? I asked her just to be sure.

She didn't get mad at the question, just said, "Here's the procedure for having the police at a ransom handover. We watch, and only act if either someone is going to get hurt, or if no one will get hurt. And we record the entire thing."

"So, I knew about the recording?" It wasn't a lie exactly. If I'd thought about it, I would have guessed. "Okay. I can do that."

She moved back. "Thanks. I owe you a big one."

SIXTY-THREE

The treatment didn't take long. A few pain pills and a set of instructions to get a lot of rest and go to my doctor tomorrow.

I called a cab from the lobby. They'd taken me to VGH and there was no way I could walk home from there.

It was hard not to feel sorry for myself. Hurt and alone waiting to go home where there was no one to take care of me. I knew it didn't help. I'd been in this situation often enough. The difference this time was that Jake was out of town, Lu and Matthieu were god knows where and Val was in sulk.

My phone rang, saving me from a full-fledged pity party. It was Val.

"Leigh called me. Are you okay? We'll come get you."

Did it make me a bad person that I was happy she felt guilty? "I'm taking a cab. I'll be fine. I just need to sleep." *At least until four a.m. when Jake will make me feel better.* "Where have you been?"

"Yeah... Um. I guess I shouldn't have been such a bitch. I did what you said. We talked it out."

That was a relief. Now I only had to help Lu's love life. "And?"

"We're moving into the guest house at Rance's place." I could hear some lingering reluctance.

"It's perfect, Val. You can still get around to your clients. You'll have a nice place to live." I stopped talking. Listing off the benefits wouldn't get her to accept the generosity of her boyfriend's dad. She'd have to live there and experience it.

"Okay, enough about me. I'll come over tomorrow with breakfast. Hey, what about that dog?"

"Mickey?" He was my last problem to deal with on this case. "He's at the vet. I'm waiting to hear if Iain's sister wants him."

"Oh." The single syllable echoed with disappointment.

"I'm guessing the answer will be no." I crossed my fingers. It was good to know they still worked. "Do you and Rory want him?"

"If no one else does." Val was trying to be causal, but I could tell by the quick response that it meant something more than just an impulse to her.

It would be good for Val to have a dog. Someone who was unlikely to leave her and would love her just for being there.

"I'll probably know tomorrow." My phone signaled a second call. "Hang on."

"No. I'll go." She hung up.

The other call was Lu. It felt good to have contact with everyone again. "Hey. Are you back?"

"No. Val called." There was a lot of noise in the background. Ringing bells and cheering.

So, Val got through but not me? I couldn't raise any emotion around that, probably due to the painkillers. "Where are you?"

"Are you okay?"

"I will be. Answer the question."

"Okay, here's the story. We are in Vegas. We got married. It was your idea to elope." The words flowed out fast enough that I couldn't quite react.

"You were supposed to invite me." I saw a cab pull up. "You could have left me a message."

"Sorry. Matthieu found a flight and we had less than fifteen minutes to pack. I really am sorry."

"When will you be back? You are going to throw a huge reception party for everyone who wanted to be there." I got in the cab and gave him the address.

"That won't be a problem. The ceremony was always the sticking point. We'll be back late tonight. I'll come over with breakfast in the morning."

Everyone wanted to feed me, and I was happy to let them. "Okay. I forgive you provisionally. You'll get the rest of it after the party. I have to go. I'm falling asleep in the cab."

I was lucky enough to get a kind driver, he made sure I was through the security gate and on my way to the house before driving away. No one was around so I got inside and set the alarm on my phone for my call with Jake before I lay on the couch and let the pills help me to sleep.

SIXTY-FOUR

I was awake before the alarm went off. I made tea and plugged my phone into the charger so a dead battery wouldn't end our call early. If I was careful not to show my arm, Jake wouldn't know how hurt I was. Of course, that was unless Val had called him too.

Right on time, my phone rang and I turned on the camera. "Hey, Babe."

Jake looked as good as he ever did, better with the tan. "Hey."

"I missed you."

He leaned in like he was looking for damage. "Val told me what happened."

"If I ever need a publicist, I'll call her. I'm fine. Really."

"No, she told me everything. You aren't fine. You're hurt, again. But you solved the case, and I know that makes up for a lot of pain."

"Yeah, I do like to win."

"I should be there to help you get better."

"It's not necessary."

He glanced down at something on the desk. "Maybe, but it's what a boyfriend would do."

"We're not kids, Jake."

"Fine. I have some news."

I already knew it would be another job. He got that look every time he announced a new gig. Like he was happy, but too sad to show it.

"A movie or a TV show?" I let him off the hook by looking as happy for him as possible. Maybe this one would be at home.

"TV show." He sucked in his top lip and I knew it wasn't a Hollywood North production.

"I'm happy for you," I lied.

"I wish it could be there, Charity. We hardly see each other anymore."

I wanted to say I missed him too. I wanted to tell him how the last two days had made me realize I needed him in my life. But I couldn't drop that on him now. This was his moment, not mine. "You can't pass up a great opportunity. Jake, you've worked really hard for this. All those bit parts and walk on roles. You deserve to be a star. We'll figure it out."

He looked down at something below the camera's range. "That's just it, Charity. I love you but this... we both know this isn't working. We haven't seen each other more than three days in the last six months." He looked up again as soon as he stopped talking. It was like he'd been reading a prepared speech. Except his eyes were shining with tears.

I had to meet him more than halfway this time. I had to be the good girlfriend. "I can get to Los Angeles more often."

"It's not in LA. It's a British production."

London. It was almost as bad as Australia. "I could..."

He shook his head. "You could what? Move away from Lu and Val?" he said it like it was impossible.

My throat was getting tight, but I managed to force out the words, "So, what now?"

"I'm tired of trying to make it work. You don't need me. I know you love me, but you just don't need me."

"I do need you. I do." I almost sobbed the words.

He looked down again. This time I could tell he was trying to get his emotions under control. That he was going to be the grown up. That there was no making deals this time.

"Charity. I can't do it anymore. We need to accept the inevitable and move on. I've asked Ilene to find a tenant for my place."

If he wasn't selling, there was hope. "I don't want to do this, Jake."

"I know, babe, but you can't just wait for me to come back. Please tell me you'll let me go."

I wanted to beg. I wanted to tell him I'd move. But that wasn't me. He was right. I didn't need him.

"I promise." It was a whisper.

"I'll call you," he said quickly. "I think we can still be friends — oh god that seems so trite, but I mean it. We need to give it time. I'll call you. I promise."

I wouldn't be able to take that.

"No, Jake. Maybe if you come back we can pick up our friendship. If you want me to move on, you have to let me go all the way. No calls. No emails. Promise?"

I could see the tears on his cheeks.

I could feel them on mine.

"If that's what it will take, then I promise."

How could a man I'd only seen a few times in the last two years leave such a giant hole in my heart. I took in a shuddering breath.

"Bye."

I hit end call and curled up on my couch, dropped my control on the pain in my chest, and let the sobs out.

WANT MORE?

Working cold cases for the VPD isn't Charity's idea of fun, but a hot case and a lot of coincidences heats up the investigation. Use the QR code to grab your copy of DREAMS.

Sneak peek on the next page.

If you enjoyed reading Avarice, please consider helping other readers to find the story by leaving a review.

CHAPTER 1

"Hey, Charity, are you around?" Val's voice floated up to the patio.

I'd given up trying to make her knock on the door like a normal person and handed her a key. That way I didn't waste energy wondering how she broke in. It's not like she was disturbing anything private in my life anyway.

"Grab a coke and come up," I said. The great thing about a tiny home is you don't need to yell. Or maybe it's just my neighborhood, where yelling gets you the wrong kind of attention.

I heard the fridge slam and then Val appeared in the door to the patio, Rory right behind her. They stepped out and grabbed a plastic chair each. I put the printout from my only actually active case face down on the table and dropped my phone on it as a paperweight.

"What are you doing?" Val asked.

She'd learned to preface her requests for favors with what appeared to be concern for other people. I looked forward to when she finally exited the self-centered teenage phase. Her history delayed her maturity but hadn't made her jaded, which was good — in the long term.

"Preparing for a case." I pushed the bowl of chips toward them. "Are you just visiting?"

"Lu and Matthieu left today, right?"

My best friend and her husband were spending the next three months in France. At least I hoped it was only that long.

"Yes," I said. "We had dinner yesterday. I've been lectured about making friends while she was gone." Seriously, you'd think I didn't know how to do those things.

"She's such a mom. Are you busy with more than that case?" She nodded toward the file.

"We winnowed the outstanding cases down," I said. "I'll be looking for more clients soon."

Val ran her own business, so she knew how hard it might be to find new clients. The personal organization consultant, as she called it, morphed occasionally as she found new interests. Currently she was working with Rory's dad to create order in their archived files.

Rory MacDonald was the only child of Vancouver's most famous and successful lawyer, Rance MacDonald. He didn't want to follow his dad's path and was trying his hand at being a documentary movie auteur. Rance had done me a few favors too, and maybe he had some cases to refer to me. It would give me something to fill my time.

"I thought maybe you wanted to go out for dinner," Val said.

Hmm, that was a first. "Lu told you to make sure I didn't spend the entire time moping?"

"Yes," Rory said. "But that's not the only reason."

"I was going to tell her our idea over dinner," Val said.

"We'll still go," Rory said. He turned to me and straightened up, going from casual semi-hipster to professional as he did. I wondered if his dad gave him some pointers.

"Charity," he said. "I, we, I mean. We were thinking about how to help you keep busy. I know you don't have much work going on and we didn't want to find you moping, that part is true."

I held up my hand to stop him. "Rory, you've got the body language down, but you need to be more focused when you talk if you want to be taken seriously."

He asked me a while back to do that. Give him feedback without sugar coating it. We shared that facet of personality. We didn't recognize hints about ourselves. We needed it blunt.

He nodded and then closed his eyes for a moment. "Thanks. I think it would do us both some good if I started following you around and filming your investigations."

"No." He couldn't be with me all the time. How would I sneak off for an afternoon of binging TV?

Val groaned. "You didn't even think about it."

"Clients won't like it. I might get sued if they see their case on the screen. I have to go into some iffy situations that would be worse if Rory were there. Informants wouldn't talk if they were on camera. Is that enough thought?"

Rory touched Val's arm to stop her from speaking again.

"All very good objections," he said. "But I would only film when we had permission. Maybe your clients would like having a visual of the investigations."

"Maybe they would, but I don't want them to learn what I do to close a case."

"I could edit out what you don't want them to see."

While Rory and I talked, Val pouted and watched the seagulls. I imagined the discussion before they came. Rory telling Val not to use emotional blackmail to get her way; Val saying I should just do what she asked. I had to give the guy credit. He would probably be a success in the film world with lots of persistence. But he thought we were still negotiating, and I planned to stand firm.

That said, I knew how to end this kind of thing. "Let me think about it."

"That's all I ask."

Now that I'd won, even though Rory thought he was still in the game, I could be magnanimous. "Where do you want to go for dinner? My treat."

It turned out the dinner was just an excuse. Rory said he had things to do and left Val with me. If I didn't know him better, I would have sworn he was sulking, but that's not how Rory did things. At a wild guess, I imagined he was off thinking of a new avenue to convince me to agree.

Val offered to make something, but I ordered pizza.

"Why don't we stay up here until it arrives?" Val asked. "It's a nice day, and you look like you could use the relaxation."

"What's the other favor?" I asked.

"Nothing. I'm just worried about you."

There was actual sincerity in her voice. Maybe she was growing up. "I'm over Jake."

"But you haven't met anyone new. You're not even trying. You aren't moving on."

I picked up my notes and started for the door. "I didn't say I was ready to date. I'm too busy with work."

Val rolled her eyes.

"Don't start with me, Val. I'll date when I'm ready. With Lu and Matthieu heading to France, I'm going to be busy with clients."

Downstairs, I dropped the papers on the counter and grabbed a beer for me and another soda for Val.

"Matthieu said you didn't have much work."

Matthieu had a big mouth. "I'll get new ones."

"Well, maybe you could come out with us some time and maybe you'll meet someone."

"I don't think I'll find someone suitable for me by hanging

out with you." I turned on the TV, hoping it would end the conversation.

"What about hanging with someone your age?" Val plopped onto the sofa beside me.

"I don't know anyone like that." I had a very small circle of friends. Two. One was on her way to France, the other was on my sofa.

Val grabbed the remote. "What about Leigh?"

"We're not friends." I appreciated her help and her ability to save my life more than once, but I was sure Leigh wouldn't think of me as a friend either.

Val stopped flicking the channels and settled on a reality show. "Try asking. Or I can invite you both over for dinner and you could get to know her better and then suggest you go to a bar or something."

"Now it sounds like you're setting us up," I said. "Just watch the show."

"Fine."

We sat unspeaking for the twenty minutes it took for the pizza to arrive. I let the guy through the security gate and met him halfway down the finger dock to pay him. Usually I waited for deliveries at my door. Tonight, I figured Val would try to set me up with him if I let him any closer.

When I got back, the show was finishing, and the news starting. Val had put plates and napkins on the coffee table.

"Let's check out a movie," she said, pulling a slice from the box.

"I want the news."

"You can watch it online. You don't have to wait for them to feed stuff to you."

If I did that, I would be too close to Facebook and Twitter. I didn't want to admit that to Val. "Let's just hear what they have to say and then we can stream a movie."

Val laughed and sat back, chewing on her pizza.

I wanted to hear if the cops had made any progress on the murder of a journalist. She fell down a staircase at the hospital. Going to the most dangerous parts of the world to get a story makes you careful, so I had a hard time believing she fell by accident. If they didn't have some kind of lead by now, it might be a hard case to solve.

"It is unclear what Ms. LaSalle was doing at the hospital," the male anchor said. "Our sources have been unable to identify any family or friends who had been admitted. The police are asking for anyone who may have seen her while at the hospital to contact them with any information. "

As usual on this channel, the other anchor needed to chip in part of the story. I guess we were supposed to think they'd done a joint investigation.

"Bob, do we know if the police contacted her employer?"

"They are refusing to give a statement," Bob answered. "It is possible that she was there in a freelance capacity."

The female anchor smiled. "I'm sure we'll have more information soon." She turned to face the camera and the image behind her changed to show a car wreck. "An accident southbound on the Oak Street Bridge delayed the commute by several hours tonight."

"It would be great if you had a case like that," Val said. "I mean, not great that someone got murdered. If Rory could document a murder case, he'd be famous right away."

"Only the cops investigate murders. Don't bother to ask, there's no way they would agree. And I won't agree to let Rory follow me around."

Val decided she'd rather spend the rest of the evening with Rory and called a cab as soon as the last slice of pizza disappeared. It gave me free time; time I should be spending on the employee espionage case, but sorting through telephone records and emails didn't appear on my list of things I wanted to do; binging a show did.

Before I found the one I wanted, my phone rang. For someone who apparently had no friends and no life, I sure had a lot of interruptions.

"Hi, Leigh," I said after checking the caller ID.

"Hey, Charity." She sounded overly cheerful. When Leigh, the police officer, called, it was more often a warning to stay away from something or a scolding for having done something. I didn't think Leigh the police detective would be much different. "Listen, I called because I heard you're at loose ends right now. I thought we could go out for a drink sometime. Maybe tomorrow?"

I sighed. "Who put you up to managing my social life?"

"Busted. Let's hope I'm better at lying to suspects than I am to anyone else. Lu said you might turn into a hermit."

Would that be bad?

"Why won't they let me be? I have recovered from breakups before."

"I don't know you that well, but if I had to guess, this one is different. I didn't even know you had a boyfriend. But since he ended it, you haven't bothered me for help, or needed me to get you out of a jam."

If even Leigh could see there was a problem, maybe I was in denial. Then again, maybe I was only being independent.

"For the record, I ended it." Not exactly the truth, but I felt better with the lie. "Okay, drinks tomorrow. Where?"

"You know Pourhouse down on Water?" she asked.

"At seven?"

"Good enough. I have an opportunity you might be interested in."

It wasn't that late, and I didn't want to wait until tomorrow. "How about in an hour instead?"

Leigh hesitated and that got me worried. "Okay, I'll make some arrangements. See you there."

Arrangements? Was this some kind of trap? Had I crossed a line lately? If the cops wanted me, they knew where I lived. I know, paranoia is not a great character trait, at least not when I'm between cases.

I was wearing jeans and an old sweatshirt since the only thing I planned was a night at home. I briefly considered not changing, but realized I'd end up being more uncomfortable than if I wore something more appropriate. After all, if Leigh needed to 'make arrangements' then I could make an effort.

A quick shower, some dressier black pants and green silk tank under a sheer pullover made me look like I might be worthy of a date. I didn't do full makeup, but a bit of blush, mascara, and lipstick helped me look alive.

I hated to admit it, but getting ready made me feel some enthusiasm for the event. I called a taxi because I didn't want to spoil the effect by walking the twenty minutes to the bar.

CHAPTER 2

Leigh got out of a cab across the street just as mine pulled away. Without her cop look, she looked five years younger. Her blond hair was loose around her face, she wore makeup too, and her clothes flattered rather than tried to hide her athletic body. Maybe I needed a few lessons on how to dress. Was it weird that I felt a flash of jealousy because guys might not notice me with her around? *Yes.*

I waved and waited for her to cross the street before heading in. The bar was half empty and lacked the desperation I remembered from the last time I hung around one at almost eleven at night.

We found a table and ordered drinks. "So, an opportunity?" I didn't want to waste time dancing around the information.

"Relax," Leigh said. "Let me start at the beginning."

"Yeah. Always the best place to start," Val said as she pulled out a chair and joined us.

"I thought you went home to Rory."

"Really? I thought you were a detective. You are so easy to lie to, Charity. I'm here because I don't trust you to listen."

Leigh called the waiter over and Val ordered a soda.

"That was my idea," Leigh said. "It's important to me, and I thought Val could help."

Everything she said sounded like proof people were ganging up on me. I could have stayed home on my couch for this. "Start talking. I actually looked forward to a night out, so your opportunity better be good."

Val and Leigh exchanged glances.

"You know I've been promoted," Leigh said.

"Yeah, to detective," I said.

"Well, it's not what I hoped. Don't get me wrong, the work is great, I just wish I got access to the important cases."

"So, you want to join our agency?" I would miss her as an asset on the force, but Leigh would bring experience to our team I didn't have, and connections Matthieu was still trying to make.

"No," Leigh said. She waved her hands as if wiping out the idea. "I like being a cop. Today, my boss offered to let me be in charge of some old cases — not cold exactly, but stalled."

"Congrats," I said. "We'll celebrate."

"No, just listen, Charity," Val said.

"You heard about that journalist, right?" Leigh said. "Well, we're under a lot of pressure to solve her murder, so most of the guys are assigned to her case. We're short staffed right now and these cases aren't low enough priority to be set aside."

"I still don't understand why I'm here." I didn't know her well, but Leigh hadn't struck me as the type to brag.

"She needs help and there aren't any other cops, or maybe they don't want to help." Val looked at Leigh as she said the last bit.

"It's not like that. I need to prove myself before I'm allowed to join the club, but no one would jeopardize a case to keep me out."

I agreed with Leigh, mostly from experience. The cops were mad at me for a while, but they still did their job. Helping me out wasn't part of the job. Cooperation came as a benefit from a relationship. I was currently working on that.

"Still don't get it," I said. Although I had an idea, I couldn't believe I would be sanctioned to help.

"I got a budget to hire a contractor," Leigh said. "I also got the okay for you to be that contractor. Unless you're too busy."

I sipped my drink to give my mouth something to do that didn't include blurting out my first thought: a solid no. Some part of my brain mentioned that I could finish the outstanding case in a few hours of detecting. The voice also reminded me that with nothing to do, I might just sit around eating and getting fat.

"You're bored, Charity," Val said, misinterpreting my silence. "You need to do something, and if it's not this, I'll start setting you up with dates and mess around in your love life."

I put down my glass. "Here's the deal. I'll help, but if there's any game-playing from the official side, I'm not holding back. Are you okay with my conditions, Leigh?"

"I prefer you not trash my career, but I don't see any way of stopping you." She looked at her watch. "I have to go. I'll see you at eight thirty tomorrow in my cubicle?"

I gave a thumbs up and Leigh left us.

"Val, you don't need to take care of me," I said.

"You say that, but you aren't doing anything to reassure us you're okay." She finished her soda and stood. "I gotta go, you should too. Get a good night's sleep and make an impression tomorrow. A good one!"

I DIDN'T OBEY VAL. I spent most of the night closing out my case and writing the report for the client. I'd give it another look over when I got home later and send it off. But I wanted to look like I fit in an office full of cops, so I needed a little sleep, a shower, and more than a little makeup for that to happen.

I met Leigh in the reception area of the police station on Cambie. It wasn't as convenient as the one on Main, but the homicide department had moved and so I wouldn't be walking to work much. This time instead of being escorted back to Leigh's desk, I filled out a form and was rewarded with a visitor badge. Until someone revoked it, I could access the station without escort at any time. I tried not to think of ways I would screw up, but all that documentation on criminals sang welcome to me as soon as the badge hung around my neck.

"Charity," Leigh said in a tone that told me she'd called me more than once. "You'll get a spare cube later, but we can start right now."

I followed her back to the bullpen, making note as she pointed out the lunchroom, bathroom, and file room.

"Will I get access to the system?"

"Visitor access," Leigh said. "Same as the file room. You won't be able to alter anything on a document, but you can look at anything that isn't classified. You can review anything in the room but won't be able to take anything out."

I didn't know if I was more disappointed I couldn't run wild and free through the police records, or relieved they had good control. "So, three cases," I said.

Leigh picked up the top file. "The oldest first. Jackson Tripton, dead by poison May 3 this year. No lover on the side, no real enemies. We cleared the wife, although she remarried only six weeks later."

"You mean no known enemies," I said. "How did you clear the wife?"

"Alibi. I know what you're going to say, but she didn't leave the poison for him to take while she had an alibi. We found an injection mark on his foot."

I thought that sounded a little too pat, but accusing the cops of being facile with a case was not the way to start out our working relationship. "Okay. Do I get a copy of the file?"

"Just don't take anything out of the office," she said, handing me the folder. "Next, we have Alex Sandhu, stabbed May 6. It looks like he was taking a morning run, and someone saw him as an easy target."

She lay the file open in front of me, the pictures were first. "Someone was angry," I said. The autopsy photo showed five wounds around his heart. "How far did you get?"

"It does look personal," Leigh said. "The investigating officer didn't make any progress. No witnesses. It was early in the morning. The knife was gone, and we only found his DNA."

These both seemed more than stale. It sounded to me like they were on the back burner from day one. "And the last one?"

"Mary Copp, not murder, yet. She was pushed off the seawall on May 17. A cyclist saw the attack and called 911. Copp is in VGH in a coma. We're hoping she'll tell us something if she comes out of it."

"The cyclist?"

"Didn't see enough detail. Only that it was definitely not an accident. The suspect is medium build, but wearing sweats and a hoodie, so he's not sure if the attacker was male or female."

"How come I haven't heard of these?" It wasn't like we were the murder capital of Canada. We still cared enough to report on deaths like this.

"They were on the news, but it was around the time of the election. All three were bumped off the front page by the stories discrediting one or the other candidate."

I checked the dates on the file. All within three weeks. Not regular spacing, the first two in the first week of May, the last right after the election was over. "Is that unusual? To have them close together?"

"Yes. We don't get many murders, but don't make a conspiracy case out of it. The brass won't appreciate you trying to sensationalize the cases."

"If conspiracy is there, we'll find it," I said. "So, what do we do first?"

It was a boring day. Leigh made me dig into the files and learn all the facts before she would even listen to an idea of how to proceed. By the end of the day, I knew everything and maybe tomorrow we could get some interviews down.

I SAT in the bar at the Bayshore waiting for Leigh to return from the bathroom. Our drink orders were on their way. That was the second bonus of working with Leigh, she liked to end the day with a bit of socializing. Matthieu and I mostly worked independently and, looking back, maybe that helped me turn into a hermit.

"Hey," Val's voice came from behind me.

I turned, and she walked up with Rory and grabbed a chair to join us. "How did you know I was here?" It wasn't like Val to just drop into a bar...or at least I didn't think so.

"I called them," Leigh said, sliding into her chair.

This was starting to feel like a set up. "Why?" I tried not to sound suspicious, but I didn't like feeling maneuvered.

Leigh took her drink from the waiter. "We've been given orders."

"You weren't supposed to tell her," Val said, slumping into the chair.

"Babe, Charity's not stupid. She already figured it out." Rory ordered two sodas and sat back in the chair like he was observing a scene from a movie.

That last night at dinner, Lu had been anxious, but I thought I'd settled her mind. When she fell in love with Matthieu, I asked her not to move to France and leave me alone. When they stayed here, I said it was a joke, and it was — mostly.

"She's supposed to be thinking about herself, not worrying about me." If I ruined their extended vacation, I'd never forgive myself.

"She is," Leigh said. "That's why we agreed to keep you occupied."

"Yeah, that and you need to find something more interesting than the TV. You aren't getting younger," Val said.

I didn't respond to the comment; she was young enough that I might seem ancient. If she was trying to get a rise out of me, I wouldn't give her the satisfaction.

"Do you really need help on the cases? Or is this in aid of project Stop Charity Moping?"

"That is real," Leigh said. "I wouldn't risk my career by involving a civilian without approval. That said, I fought for you to be the consultant because you are a good investigator."

"What cases?" Val asked.

"We can't talk about them," I said before Leigh could.

"Three possible murders," Leigh said before I finished. "Or I guess, two possible murders and a definite attempted."

Val nudged Rory.

He slid a glance at me, his face flushing. "Would it help to have the investigation documented?"

Now I got the real setup. Val was going to push this until she got her way. Fortunately, this wasn't for me to shut down. Leigh could drop the official line and that would be the end.

"What do you mean?" she asked.

"So, you know I'm a documentary filmmaker," Rory said, his face losing the embarrassed flush as he got excited about his dream. "The real crime stuff is hot now. I could film you in your investigation and then edit it into a short each day for my YouTube channel."

Leigh nodded for him to continue.

"Then I'd take the highlights and create a cut for festival entries...Sundance and stuff."

"I can't authorize that," Leigh said.

"Why not?" Val asked.

"Babe," Rory said.

"Let me finish," Leigh said. "You need to learn to listen better if you want to get ahead in any business. I said I couldn't authorize it, but I can pass the request to my boss. If you can live with whatever restrictions she lays out?"

Val sat up. "What kind of restrictions? Rory can't sacrifice his art for some stupid rules."

I hid my smile by taking a drink. Val looked like she'd taken over as Rory's manager. He needed someone to be pushy for him. In my mind he was too willing to take the first answer. I knew about the film industry from being Jake's girlfriend. There was a no, and there was an absolutely not. You got the yes somewhere between the two.

"I'll find out. It won't be negotiable. We can't risk a successful prosecution to satisfy anyone's art."

Val thought it over for a few seconds. "Fair enough, when will we hear from you?"

"I'll call you tomorrow." Leigh checked the time. "I need to go soon. Charity, we should probably set up your external access to files."

"Yeah, we gotta go get ready for filming." Val, blindly confident we would bend to her will, led Rory out.

It made me happy to see her lean into him as they walked, like teenagers in love. It was an intimacy she wouldn't have been capable of not that long ago.

I paid the bill. Val had left their drinks on our tab, but the waiter had comped them anyway. It pays to come to a local place.

We headed back to my home. Leigh had some encryption to run on my laptop that would allow me to access some non-critical files from home. I think she thought I was uncomfortable at the station. I wasn't, but I liked the idea of working from my place sometimes, away from official eyes.

I logged on and left her to work while I checked my cupboards for supplies. I always had great intentions of stocking my kitchen and cooking for myself, but I never did. Jake had been my source for all things domestic, but if Leigh was going to be working here, I should have some basics.

It occurred to me that Jake only popped into my mind twice in the last hour, and there was no reminder of the aching hole where our relationship used to sit. The past felt more like a fond memory than a raw wound. Perhaps I was making progress.

"Done," Leigh said. "Do you remember your password?"

I logged in to prove I knew how to. "Are you really going to get Rory permission to film?"

"I'll try, but he might not like the rules." Leigh checked her watch again. "I have to go, Charity."

"I thought we'd make decisions together," I said. If we didn't get this clear up front, I would barge over lines without knowing. Clarity wouldn't stop me from barging, but at least I'd know I was doing it.

"We should probably talk about that tomorrow," Leigh said. "No time to discuss it now."

She didn't give me a chance to say anything to delay her, just opened my door, said 'bye' and left.

So much for partnership.

. . .

IF YOU WANT to know more, us the QR code to check out
DREAMS.

FREE EBOOK

Claim your copy of Buying Into Death when you use the QR code to sign up for my newsletter and follow Charity as she solves her fastest case yet!

ALSO BY P A WILSON

For more books by P A Wilson

Use the QR code below or go to pawilson.ca

ABOUT THE AUTHOR

Perry Wilson is a Canadian author based in Vancouver, BC who has big ideas and an itch to tell stories. Having spent some time on university, a career, and life in general, she returned to writing in 2008 and hasn't looked back since (well, maybe a little, but only while parallel parking).

She is a member of the Vancouver Writers Social Group, The Royal City Literary Arts Society, and The Surrey Writing Workshop. Perry has self-published several novels. She writes the Madeline Journeys, a fantasy series about a high-powered lawyer who finds herself trapped in a magical world, the Quinn Larson Quests, which follows the adventures of a wizard named Quinn who must contend with volatile fae in the heart of Vancouver, and the Charity Deacon Investigations, a mystery thriller series about a private eye who tends to fall into serious trouble with her cases, and The Riverton Romances, a series based in a small town in Oregon, one of her favorite states. Her stand-alone novels are Breaking the Bonds, Closing the Circle, and The Dragon at The Edge of The Map.

For more information
www.pawilson.ca
pawilson@pawilson.ca

f X

ACKNOWLEDGMENTS

People think that the process of writing is solitary. That's not the case for me. I have help from so many people it would be hard to acknowledge everyone, but I'll give it a try.

The support and inspiration I get from my writer's groups is incalculable. The Vancouver Writers Social Group opens my mind to other ways of telling a story. The Royal City Literary Arts Society gives me the opportunity to meet and share with other writers who have more knowledge than I do. The Other 11 Months group is where I learn about getting the words on the page. And my critique group who helps me find the best parts of the story I want to tell. Thanks to all of the members of these great groups.

Last of all, but definitely a huge part of the process, my beta readers. These are the people who love stories and are willing, and more than able, to tell me if my finished story is ready for you, my readers.